STALK

STALK

A NOVEL OF SUSPENSE

LOUIS CHARBONNEAU

DONALD I. FINE, INC.

NEW YORK

Library of Congress Cataloging-in-Publication Data

Charbonneau, Louis, 1924–
Stalk / Louis Charbonneau.
p.   cm.
ISBN 1-55611-284-X
I. Title.
PS3575.O7S7   1992
813'54—dc20   91-58660
CIP

Manufactured in the United States of America

10 9 8 7 6 5 4 3 2 1

Designed by Irving Perkins Associates

This one is for
Sue and Dave,
Barbara and Roger,
Debbie and Gary
with love

STALK

1

COMING UP THE WALK toward the broad front porch—a California cottage, the realtor had called it, built in the early 1930s—
McLean wasn't remembering the phone call, or the disturbing
sense that something had been wrong last night with Angie.
Instead he was remembering a fragment of conversation from the
night, and a smile relieved the hardness of his features.

"What people don't realize," she had said, "is that spies get
old, too. If you would just let everyone in on your secret, you'd
get more sympathy."

"I don't need sympathy," he said. "I'm not old. And I'm not
a spy."

"You used to be. And you're getting gray. Your chest hair
has all this gray in it, see? And down there, I saw a couple of
gray hairs."

"You weren't supposed to be looking." His hand stroked her
bare shoulder, marveling as always at the velvet smoothness.

11

"And your beard. I admit it's distinguished, those two white streaks coming down here on each side of your mouth . . ." Her lips nibbled at each corner of his mouth in turn. "But I bet you'd look ten years younger if you shaved it off."

"Five, maybe."

"Ten. Ten easy."

"Forty-four isn't so old."

"Prove it," she said.

McLean was still smiling when he unlocked the front door, but he paused in the dim foyer, the smile fading. By some subliminal perception he knew even in that instant that neither Angie nor the boy was there. Not that they were out of the house. That they were gone, leaving an emptiness that struck him with physical pain, like the deep cold of a house long abandoned in winter.

But the house wasn't empty.

He started to turn, too late, the long-unused antennae vibrating a warning, the reflexes slower than they once were, not quite quick enough. The men moved in from two sides, and he had time for a feeling of dismay that he hadn't heard them or sensed their presence in time. *The organ of language is not vision*, a voice came to him from the past; *the organ of language is the ear*. The organ of survival, too, he had thought then, and proved to himself a score of times. But that organ had become dulled from minimal use.

They were pros of their kind. The bigger man was as tall as McLean but much heavier, the size of a defensive end. He had curly black hair, a flattened upper lip and broken nose, small brown eyes with an eager, innocent expression. His companion was leaner, sharper, smaller. His eyes were gray and very cold, the color of winter in the ghetto. His ears lay flat against his skull and were covered by lank blond hair grown unfashionably

long. He was more detached and, McLean thought, more dangerous. He said, "Where is she, Redfern?"

"You tell me."

The big man tipped him around with an almost casual pressure
on one shoulder and slammed a forearm into McLean's jaw.
McLean saw the blow coming but there was no way to duck or
evade it. The best he could do was try to ride with the punch,
taking it on his cheekbone while his head was moving. But he
was too constricted in his movement. The blow landed hard.
McLean felt the flesh tear. His brain sloshed around in his skull,
colliding with bone and blackness. While he was sagging the
second assailant, whose small thin body was all corded muscle,
delivered a vicious blow to McLean's kidneys.

The survival instinct took over. At least that hadn't completely
eroded. It warned him—there was no reasoning involved, simply
a flash of intuition—to be what he had been publicly these past
three years, just an average guy, nothing special, no one to be
noticed, the kind of man easily destroyed by any pair of reasonably competent musclemen with a couple of punches. He let
himself fall and curled into a helpless fetal position.

The football player kicked him in the head and for a little
while McLean was whirling through space without a space suit.
He wasn't sure how long it was before he began to drift back
down to earth.

Voices a long way off. The big man's rumble did most of the
talking. The little guy didn't say much. In fact he hadn't done
much but McLean could still feel that kidney punch. He hoped
there wasn't too much damage.

Fists, he thought. Feet. The two men were professionals but
of another breed than he was. Or had been once. This discovery
told him something but he was not sure how much. Most of the
input was negative: It told him what these men were *not*. They

were not from his world, the one he had once inhabited and left behind so long ago now that he had thought the break complete, final, forever. In that world fists and feet were too slow, too clumsy, too vulnerable.

"You shouldn't have axed him," the smaller man said, sounding closer now. "How's he gonna tell us anythin' if you take his ear off and he can't listen?"

"He was mouthin' us, man. Maybe he's tough."

"Yeah? So what does he sell, insurance? How tough can he be?"

"He moved fast," the big man said. It was an academic discussion, without rancor. The men were not in a hurry. McLean decided that the skinny one was from the East, New York or New Jersey, but his oversized companion had the Midwest far back in his nasal tones. None of this seemed very important, but he thought about it as if it were.

"Yeah. Well, he ain't movin' very fast now, is he?"

McLean tried to concentrate on as many details as possible. He had an idea that things would get worse—they wanted something from him that he couldn't give them, and wouldn't even if he could—and that after a while he wouldn't be able to think as clearly or to remember what he had seen. Eyes closed, he took note of the big man's pale green windbreaker that was like a golf jacket, his deck shoes, the way the sun had darkened an already coarse complexion, the sports shirt open at the neck to gold chains and a mat of black chest hair. A California boy, Duncan thought. Or maybe Las Vegas. Sun worshipper. Worked out on the Nautilus equipment. His sidekick was harder to place except for the Eastern accent. He wore an expensive suit, gray pinstripe, not off a rack. His black shoes were fine Italian leather, well polished. Patterned blue shirt, navy knit tie. His skin was sallow. Either he didn't like the sun as much as his partner or he was from some place other than the Sun Belt.

Redfern, he thought. The name on his mailbox, the name in the telephone book. So they didn't know who he really was.

They wanted *her*. Angie. It had nothing to do with him.

He contemplated this discovery with rising incredulity.

"Hey. Hey, you!" The big man picked him up as if he were a rag doll and shook him. "Wake up!"

McLean blinked his eyes open, stared stupidly.

"Where is she?"

"I . . . I don't know," McLean mumbled.

A huge fist came straight at his jaw and exploded into a fireball. McLean thought the smaller man might have protested again but he wasn't sure of anything except that the football player was angry.

When the blackness came it was welcome.

Consciousness seeped in like the light from the front part of the house. It was a while before McLean was able to separate the blackness in his brain from the dark of the room where he lay. Night, he thought. He had arrived home about six. Two hours or more? Had he been out that long?

He could hear voices, still far away, a murmuring. Gradually he was able to attach the voices to the two men who had been waiting for him in the house.

Where was Angie?

He kept his body very still and moved only his head, curious to find out if it was still attached to his body. The lance of pain made the effort seem a bad idea but he managed to look left and right, confirming that he was alone. He relaxed and probed with his senses, cataloging what he found—arms, wrists, hands, thighs, knees, feet, all the right parts in the right places, all intact.

All free to move, which didn't make much sense at first.

Obviously they weren't worried about him. He hadn't given them any reason to be. But that didn't explain why they would leave him unattended in a back room without tying him up.

Laughter came from the front of the house. A party, he thought. California Boy's rumble was louder than the rest of the laughter. McLean realized the two carefree studs were watching television. A night at home in the suburbs. What were they enjoying? "Cosby"? Reruns of "Family Ties"? "Cheers"?

He lifted his head a little further. Down at the foot of the bed, balanced on a corner of the mattress a few inches from his left ankle, was a glass of water, two-thirds full.

McLean regarded it almost with affection. The water glass explained why they had left him alone and unconscious on the bed. If he came to and moved—if he stirred at all—the glass would spill over the edge onto the hardwood floor with a clatter. Such meticulous measures suggested something else as well. They didn't want any marks on him other than the split lip he already had, which could be explained by a fall. There weren't to be any rope burns or fibers, or evidence of tape pasted over his mouth.

They expected him to be found.

McLean's brain was beginning to function, but he was not ready to trust his body. He lay still, flexing muscles, sending messages to his extremities. While he did so he put some pieces of the puzzle together very slowly.

He had known something was wrong last night when Angie took the phone call. She had stepped from the kitchen when the phone rang, anticipating his slower response—most calls were for her anyway. She was friendly, responsive, well liked in the small seaside town of Fortune, where McLean was a more private person, reticent and skeptical. There was something sensuous about her stance, hipshot against the edge of the littered secretary in a corner of the dining room, and McLean watched her with admiration. As she listened she glanced over her shoulder at him, smiling mechanically. "Yes, of course," she murmured. "I understand."

She had her long black hair pulled up, piled high in a style that looked more careless than it was. A few strands had worked loose to fall over her forehead. She brushed at them, and he saw that she was sweating.

It was a warm evening. She wore a white sleeveless top over the faded blue jeans. The setting sun shone through the window behind her, and he could see the fine golden hairs on her brown arms, the glossy sleekness of her bare shoulders. She had an olive skin that tanned easily and deeply in the California sun, giving her body a burnished smoothness that never failed to stir a response in him.

She was conscious of his stare and averted her head. The gesture was small, natural, seemingly unimportant, but McLean noted the tension behind it with the trained habit of perception that had never left him.

"Yes, thank you," she said, almost in a whisper. "I know what to do."

McLean smiled. If he hadn't known better, he could easily have interpreted the guarded conversation, the suggestion of secretiveness as signs of betrayal. How would a woman talk to a secret lover while another man listened? Just so. Very carefully—tag line of an old joke.

So he had said nothing, and when she went back into the kitchen he had not questioned her about the phone call. Lying in the bed now, he realized that there had been many questions he had not asked in the past two years, almost as if he were afraid of the answers. Just as she had not inquired into the mystery of McLean's past, accepting only that part of it which he had chosen to reveal. Somehow, without anything being said, they had accepted the fact of mutual privacy, of questions unasked. What they had was enough.

That night Angie had come to him in bed with a frenzy that he saw now as desperation, as if she knew that it might be the last time. There had not been the slow and subtle teasings both enjoyed, the withdrawals and returns that delayed and heightened sexual tension. Instead, a feverish coupling. They might have been strangers.

The big man guffawed in the living room. Behind his outburst, group laughter. Not canned, McLean thought. Live. It was Thursday evening. "The Cosby Show."

"Go check on lover boy."

"Innaminute."

"He oughta be wakin' up." New Jersey was getting impatient.

"He's not goin' anywhere. I wanta see this."

McLean sat up on the bed, taking the strain in his stomach muscles, not moving his legs or rocking the bed. He did it as slowly as he dared, and when the water glass rocked and tipped over he reached down and caught it. The water seeped soundlessly into the sheets and mattress.

He slipped his stockinged feet—they had removed his shoes—into a battered old pair of moccasins he kept by the side of the bed.

The window at the back of the bedroom was open six inches but McLean gave it no more than a passing thought. It was a wood-framed, double-hung window, old and tight. It couldn't be opened further without being heard.

The sliding door of the closet was open. Rungs of a ladder were attached to the back wall. McLean eased up the ladder and cautiously raised the partition overhead. He set it down soundlessly and went up through the opening. Just as carefully as he had removed it, he replaced the panel.

The attic darkness was relieved only by an oblong of light from a vent panel at the far end. McLean scuttled toward it, moving crablike along the ceiling joists, making little sound. He was as always surprised at how clean the unused attic was. Angie would never climb up here, afraid of spiders or mice or whatever, but there were no cobwebs to brush McLean's face in the dark, not even much dust.

The vent opening looked out on the roof of the garage. The vent panel itself was set loosely in place. McLean had it in his hands and was already leaning through the opening when he heard a bellow of rage from below.

He thrust head and shoulders through the vent opening and threw the framed panel as far as he could. It struck the edge of the garage roof, bounced out and smashed onto the driveway below.

Even before it landed McLean was scurrying back through the attic toward the closet ladder. He had to gamble that the noise from outside would draw both men out of the house—they couldn't risk letting him get away.

He threw the closet panel aside and dropped through the opening, ignoring the ladder. He landed in a crouch, his whole body taut.

The bedroom was dark. He was dealing with professionals all right. Whoever had come to the room and discovered his absence had had the quick presence of mind to leave the room in darkness, a precaution against a shot from outside. They would have searched the room, but they couldn't be sure he didn't have a weapon they hadn't found.

And the room was empty.

Swiftly McLean moved toward the living room. An explosion of laughter greeted him. Lights still on, TV set blaring. Alex was putting down his sister on "Family Ties," the dark-haired one whose looks reminded McLean a little of a younger Angie.

The wall switches were across the room from him, near the front hallway. No way he could cross the lighted room and reach them alive.

There was silence outside now. They knew they had been duped, knew he had to be inside the house. But they couldn't be sure he wasn't armed now and dangerous.

McLean had never wanted to keep a gun in the house, especially with the boy there. Now he faced two men, heavy pros, armed with handguns and God knew what else, and all he had was a growing rage.

McLean didn't want to give them too much time to think. They might simply set fire to the house or start shooting through the thin walls. They could do whatever they wanted without being stopped. They would have checked out police and fire response time. They would know how long it would take for one of the town's three police cars to get here. They might even have arranged something to make certain that those three cars were far enough away to give them leeway. A little auto accident maybe, something involving kids, something bad enough to make routine alarms seem unimportant, easily ignored at least for a little while until you wanted to get away from the immediate horror.

McLean went in a circle through the back hall and the kitchen to the front of the house. In the kitchen he spotted a utility knife on the counter. He scooped it up and carried it into the front hallway. From there, without exposing himself, he was able to reach the wall switches just inside the living room. He hit them both and plunged the house into darkness.

The sudden silence was deafening.

He waited. After a moment he heard the faint creak of a board on the porch outside the front door as someone shifted his weight. California Boy, McLean guessed. Not in front of the door where he might be vulnerable but off to the left, hidden in the shadows. If McLean tried to go through that door, he wouldn't even get it all the way open before bullets splintered the wood and plucked at his flesh.

He had to find the other one. On a hunch McLean returned to the kitchen and stood at the edge of the counter near the window. The seconds ticked by—he could hear the rhythmic ticking of the quartz clock on the wall behind the tiny dinette table. His assailants had put out one street light, the one directly in front of the house, but not the one that was halfway down the block. Its dim glow was enough to provide a faint backlight. McLean stared out at the motionless shadows.

It didn't take long. A man under tension could seldom hold his position long without shifting weight, letting out a held breath, scratching his nose. What McLean saw was an arm reaching up to brush lank hair away from a forehead. New Jersey.

That was all McLean was waiting for. He ran back to the front hallway and without hesitating threw a weighted glass ashtray through the front window with all his strength. Glass exploded outward, showering the porch and the shrubbery beyond it. While the splinters were in the air, lancing out from the center of the explosion, McLean raced back through the house and went out the kitchen door in a rush.

New Jersey had turned toward the action at the front of the house. He started to spin around when he heard the kitchen door open, but before he could bring the gun in his hand around McLean was on him. He struck with the hard edge of his good hand, the right hand. The chopping blow missed the gunman's throat but its impact buckled his knees. His gun slipped from nerveless fingers. He tried to react, to duck away, but that first harsh blow had immobilized him. McLean's second strike was more deliberate and did not miss. The lethal edge of his hand caught the thin man under his chin in the soft, vulnerable throat, driving his Adam's apple inward, crushing his windpipe.

The two blows required only as many seconds. McLean did not take time to try to recover the gun from the ground. He knew he didn't have that much time. He launched himself in a dive toward the bushes at the front of the house. He shifted the kitchen knife from left hand to right.

He hit the ground on his left shoulder, his fall broken by the junipers he had planted last summer at a corner of the porch. The staccato drumming of a machine pistol hammered at the brush over his head. He rolled and came around and saw the streaking muzzle flashes of another round. The shots were behind him but he knew a third burst would not miss. He threw the knife without aiming, calling on forgotten skills of eye and hand and arm, the skills you didn't have to think about because if you had to think they were no longer useful to you. The plastic knife handle suddenly protruded from the big man's left eye, which was not where McLean had aimed it instinctively—too easy to hit bone anywhere around the head, to cut but fail to maim or kill, leaving the adversary able to strike back. But the throw had been a lucky one.

The killer screamed, stumbling backward, clawing at his face and the terrible pain of the freak hit.

McLean scooped up the automatic weapon the big man had dropped. Coldly he fired one short burst, stitching the bullets neatly across the screaming man's chest.

He stopped screaming, and the night was suddenly, terribly silent.

2

UP AND DOWN THE STREET lights began popping on. A voice rose here and there, questioning, frightened, angry, wondering. Was no place safe any longer?

McLean did not even consider waiting, trying to offer explanations he did not have. He was accepted as a respectable citizen of the town, no trouble, quiet, kept to himself, lived with that dark-haired beauty and her kid, worked for the insurance. He would be believed when he said that two armed men had attacked him, that he had fought back only to save his own life.

But after a while the questions would be raised. Who was he? What kind of a man, armed only with a kitchen knife, could destroy two professional killers with guns, one of them an automatic weapon? And why had they come after *him*?

What's more, if he stayed he would remain a sitting duck. Two hit men looking for Angie had stayed to interrogate and then kill him. They had failed. Others would come to finish the job. No law would be able to protect him.

He didn't know who they were, who had sent them or why, but he knew enough not to wait and see. At least he would be a moving target.

For the past three years he had kept an escape kit in the garage, concealed by a false panel at the bottom of a large wooden toolbox he had bought at a garage sale. He had stained and artificially aged the extra panel to match the rest of the wood. He had almost forgotten the kit was there. Inside it were things he had not turned in when he retired—two sets of false identity papers and supporting documents, an unregistered Beretta automatic with two extra clips of ammunition, the key to a safety deposit box in Newport Beach, California, two stacks of fifties and hundreds totaling two thousand dollars, a small black notebook with names and numbers that read like a Baedeker of the world's exotic places.

He wondered suddenly if the notebook was in any way related to this night attack. He shook off the question. Angie had nothing to do with his past, and she had known the muscle was coming. Besides, there was no time for speculation. People were in the street now, some of them drifting hesitantly toward his house, reassured by the continuing silence.

The two dead men had carried no identification, but there were keys to a car in the right-hand jacket pocket of the man on the front porch with the row of bullet holes where the seeping blood had pooled. The keys identified the car as a Buick.

McLean went out a back window as the first neighbors appeared out front, gingerly inching forward across the lawn to peer at the figure sprawled across the porch. "There's another one over here!" a voice said excitedly. "By the side door." Somewhere in the night a siren wailed, its cry spilling closer.

McLean carried his escape kit, thrust into a small canvas overnight bag along with an extra shirt and set of underwear, a golf jacket, a pair of brown crepe-soled shoes, a change of socks, a small transistor radio. He trotted silently across the damp grass of the back yard, vaulted the fence and broke into a run as he reached the alley.

He found the Buick parked on the next street in a corner of the gas station lot, where it appeared as if it had been left overnight for service. The patrol car screamed past the service station as McLean turned the key and the Buick's engine fired. He waited for the police car to skid around the corner into his street before he pulled out of the station and turned right.

He drove without undue speed, lights on, turning at the first intersection in the direction of the expressway that bypassed the town on the inland side.

It would take the police time to identify the two dead men. Most likely they would have to send their fingerprints to the FBI's National Crime Information Center in Washington. There was a good chance the prints would be on file—experienced muscle like the two McLean had fought didn't reach their level of expertise without getting into trouble somewhere along the way.

There was nothing in the car to identify them. The car itself might be stolen, but McLean doubted it. For their own security on a job the car would be clean; it wouldn't be on any wanted list.

But it would be known to someone else. For that reason it would not be safe transportation for long. Just long enough for McLean to get clear. He would have to abandon it where his trail would not easily be followed. A large city, probably at an airport.

By daybreak, not stopping, he could reach San Francisco.

* * *

Driving southward through the night along the almost deserted expressway, McLean acknowledged to himself that he had not once looked back at the house where he had made a life for the past three years, two of them with Angie and the boy.

Without her it held nothing for him.

Now, he knew, the unasked questions had to be asked. In the emptiness of the night there was no evading them.

The first time he had seen her, more than two years ago, was in a supermarket. He had a glimpse of a young woman at the end of one aisle, felt an unaccustomed tingling of interest, and in spite of himself made a point of looking for her as he threaded the aisles. When he saw her heading for one of the checkout counters he abandoned half of his shopping list and managed to get behind her with his cart.

About then he asked himself what the hell he was doing. The baby had something to do with those second thoughts. A boy, he rode in the cart on the red plastic flip-down seat. Dark eyes studied McLean with sober, unwavering interest. After a while McLean smiled. The boy responded instantly, grinning back at him and cocking his head. As McLean would later learn, he was a sunny-tempered child. His mother, who appeared to pay no notice, instead watching the cash register closely as her items were rung up, gave a faint smile, a glance too brief for McLean to read anything in it.

Moments later she wheeled car and baby and groceries out of the market while McLean stood at the checkout counter, staring after her, wondering why the tingling persisted.

Oh, there were enough good reasons to stare at her—at least a half-dozen other men did the same before she reached the yellow Volkswagen in the parking lot. She was wearing light beige slacks, a smooth polyester knit that clung to long and shapely legs. Her legs were the only feature with which she would admit satisfaction. Like most beautiful women she found fault with the rest of her figure. Her breasts were too small, her shoulders sloping, her waist too long, her hips too wide. Her viewpoint; McLean never agreed. At that first meeting he was left with an impression of a woman of extraordinary sensual appeal of which she seemed quite unconscious. His mind automatically registered details as if filling out an identification sheet. Young, mid-twenties. Five feet six, a hundred and fifteen pounds. (Close. The scare point in her periodic dieting binges was a hundred twenty.) Long black hair with only a slight wave to it. Large smoke-colored eyes. Nose long and slender-bridged. Lips full with very sharp spear points at each corner. Italian or Mediterranean background (she had got her hair and coloring from her Greek mother). Good carriage, almost like a model's; the torso erect, the back straight, only the hips and legs moving when she walked, which had something to do with all those stares across the parking lot. Oh yes: add one baby, about a year old, which meant a young and jealous husband in the background. So forget it, McLean. Go home and have a cold shower.

Over the next few months he saw her several times, on the street or in the market, once at the bank and another time in the lobby of the town's only movie house. He began to look forward to these chance glimpses, and it occurred to him that she was not as oblivious of him as it appeared, as if some unspoken relationship had already sprung up between them. Whenever he saw her a smile started inside him, though it never reached his habitually expressionless face.

—*Oh, I knew you were interested.*
—*How did you know?*
—*Your eyes.*

What made all of this more remarkable was that McLean had

long ago come to terms with loneliness, with the solitary bed, the morning coffee in an empty, silent kitchen, the unused emotions locked up and the key thrown away. He considered himself a physical and emotional cripple. Physically he would never walk without a slight limp. He would never wake on a damp morning without the ache in his restructured knee and in the three enlarged knuckles of his left hand, the fingers that would never completely make a fist or even close around the grip of a golf club. Emotionally he knew that most people thought him cold, hard, without feeling. If it was not an internal reality, it was a self-fulfilling facade.

Three months passed before McLean spoke to the dark-haired woman. By then, of course, he knew quite a bit about her. Fortune was a small town, people talked, and McLean was a good listener. Once a booming lumber town on the northern California coast south of Eureka, Fortune—named for its glory days—was now a tranquil place, enjoying a brief flurry of tourists during the summer months but afterward settling into misty quiet. In such a town there was no way Angela Simmons was going to go unnoticed or unmentioned. McLean learned that the boy, Anthony, was her only child; that there was no visible husband, a fact that occasioned some gossip; that she worked at the local high school library; that she drove an elderly yellow Volkswagen with a sunroof; that she rented a small garage apartment on the east side of town from the Harrisons, who owned the property and lived in the main house; that most of the students at Fortune High thought she was "neat."

By the end of those first months McLean was no longer able to laugh off the quivering in his gut whenever he saw her. He also told himself that it was impossible. He wasn't a schoolboy. During his three years in Fortune everything had worked out as planned. He liked the town, he had attuned himself to its placid pace, he had a job as an insurance appraiser that brought in an adequate income, and enough time had gone by for him to permit himself to believe that those who still nurtured a lethal hatred of him would have stopped actively searching. There was no way he would jeopardize all that by getting involved with a woman for more than a few hours—and Angela Simmons was no one-night stand.

They met on an autumn afternoon during halftime at the high school football game. Fortune was playing Gold Bluff and losing. She was in line at the hot dog stand behind the tiered seats when McLean came up behind her. He had a momentary impulse to turn on his heel and walk away. He didn't.

It was an overcast day, cool with the usual threat of rain along this coastline in the fall, and she wore a light trenchcoat loose over her shoulders. McLean stared at the back of her head, at the glossy black hair and the slender neck, and felt the slow, strong surge of the response he had been denying for so long. He also felt a tension from her, as if she flinched from his reaction.

For a full two minutes they stood that way, shuffling forward toward the counter, before she turned. The impact of her stare was physical. McLean knew that what he was feeling was there for her to see.

Her lips parted but she didn't smile. Her gaze was very sober, reminding him of her son's. It was a difficult decision for her too, he thought, and wondered why.

He spoke abruptly, memorable words they would laugh at later. "Mustard and relish?"

When she nodded he stepped past her to the counter, bought two hot dogs and two paper cups of black coffee. She shook her head at cream or sugar. He smeared mustard and relish onto the weiners and handed one to her along with the coffee. Then he said, "But no onions." She laughed for the first time, and he was lost.

Two weeks later Angie and Tony moved into the clapboard California cottage with him. McLean felt that he could date the beginning of his life from that afternoon, as if nothing before it mattered.

But he had been wrong.

Hurtling along the highway through the darkness, passing a solitary truck carrying Washington apples and onions to southern markets, alone again with the twin spears of his headlights, the rush of night air from the open window cool against his face, McLean had the sense of rushing back in time, not only into his own past but toward Angie's.

In leaving Fortune as he had, leaving the carnage behind him, he was breaking the rules, violating the promise he had made to the Agency. ("We can't be responsible for what happens if you come out," Zeller had said, the quiet words coming with a sting of unmistakable warning.)

But it was not his past that had caught up with him. It was Angie's.

And for McLean that was almost a total blank.

3

ON THE OUTSKIRTS OF OAKLAND McLean pulled into a twenty-four-hour coffee shop. It was still dark outside. He sat at a booth by himself in a corner and methodically, without pleasure or awareness of what he was eating, downed bacon and eggs, the ubiquitous hash browns and toast. The potatoes were dry, the toast buttered sparsely in the center. There were little plastic cups of mixed fruit jelly with the toast. None of this mattered, but eating, storing up energy, keeping his mind alert, that did matter.

"More coffee?"

McLean nodded. The waitress sloshed some of it over the rim of the cup into the saucer, shrugged and walked away. Have a nice day.

McLean absently folded his napkin into a square and put it under his cup, soaking up the spilled coffee. Whatever else was wrong, this was one coffee shop that would survive. The coffee

was rich and strong and smooth. Not bitter. You sound like a
TV commercial, McLean thought.

By the third cup he had confirmed the decision already
reached on his long drive. There had never been any doubt that
he would try to follow Angie, try to track her down. The only
question had been whether or not he would break the terms of
his three-year exile and call in to the Agency.

They would find out soon enough that he had departed Fortune
in a hurry, and that he had left a litter of violence behind him.
Better to hear it, and whatever explanation he had to offer, from
him.

He took his time, and light was breaking in the east when he
left the coffee shop. The morning cloud layer was so thick it was
like a fine drizzle, and he had to turn on the windshield wipers.
The rhythmic thumpety-thump of the wiper blades provided a
melancholy background for his thoughts. *Why did you run, Angie? Why couldn't you trust me to take care of you?*

She had always turned aside any questions about her past.
"All that matters is what we have now," she had said once.

"And the future."

"Goes without saying," she said with a laugh and a toss of
her long hair over her shoulder.

Perhaps even then she had not dared count on the future.

The only time he had ever asked her a blunt question about
her marriage had come one night when they were watching a
made-for-TV movie about a battered wife. McLean glanced over
during one violent scene and saw Angie hugging her arms,
gooseflesh prickling the skin as she shivered.

Afterwards he had asked, "Did he beat you?"

Surprise flicked in her gray eyes like a silvery fish darting
from the depths of a pool. "How did you know?" She glanced
toward the television screen. "Was I that obvious?"

"Yes. Was Tony abused, too? Is that why you ran?"

Angie shook her head. "Forget it, honey. It's over. It has nothing to do with us . . ."

Not over, McLean thought grimly. But would an angry ex-husband send two killers after her? Or to retrieve the boy? Or was the secret of her past even darker, more mysterious than he could guess?

The questions followed him to the airport, where he left the Buick in a parking garage after wiping off the steering wheel and door handles. He bought a PSA ticket on the next commuter flight to Los Angeles, paying cash and using one of the cover names salvaged from his escape kit. No one asked him for identification.

Everything he had brought with him was in his canvas carry-all, which was small enough to stow under the seat. He had left the parts of the Beretta, broken down into pieces, in three separate trash receptacles—at a gas station along the highway, at the coffee shop where he had had breakfast, and in the men's room of the airline before he went through the security check.

He made his phone call from an open booth in the terminal, cupping his exposed ear against the blare of announcements of impending flights. The area code was for Langley, Virginia.

A crisp voice answered, giving only a phone number. McLean smiled thinly as he recognized the voice and three years vanished like vapor in the sun. "John Wesley," McLean said. It wasn't his name or even a code name, but one that Thornton had pinned on him once when they worked together. It was a private code. At least McLean hoped it was. John Wesley Hardin, gunman extraordinary, man of many notches. Real name Bernard, call me Barney.

"Jesus," Thornton breathed into the mouthpiece.

"Risen." The shorthand humor of the reply was meant more as a confirmation of identity than anything else. Three years was a long time.

"My God, Barney, what have you been up to? It came in on the wire last night and I saw it first thing this morning. The police out there didn't know anything about you, but there's someone with the insurance agency who has a flag on your file . . ."

"I wondered how you got me the job," McLean said.

"You shouldn't have run."

"What else was I going to do?" McLean answered dryly. "I shouldn't have killed them either, but the alternative was unacceptable."

"For Chrissakes, Barney, *who the fuck were they?*"

McLean listened closely. He thought Thornton's note of panic was genuine enough. "I don't know. But they weren't after *me*, Paul. That's why I had to leave. And that's why I need the answers to some questions—and I need them fast."

"I can't help you, Barney," Thornton said quickly. "You know that. I shouldn't even be talking to you now."

"You've got to, Paul. There's nobody else."

There was a long silence. McLean could hear the whispers of other conversations on the long-distance line. Paul Thornton was a company man in every sense, loyal and dependable and not too ambitious. In his brief tour of field duty he had been a reliable backup, not an adventurer, and early in his career he had gravitated naturally to a desk. But McLean had saved his life once, when an operation had backfired and Thornton had been pushed unexpectedly into the line of fire. He had been the best man at Thornton's wedding, the godfather at the christening of his first daughter, Linda. McLean fancied he could hear his old friend's personal loyalty quarreling with his duty to the Agency, like those thin voices clashing across the miles of cable and light beams . . .

Thornton sighed. "What is it you need to know, Barney?"

"I've been living with a woman for the past two years."

"I know. That much is in your file. I was glad for you."

McLean nodded to himself. Of course they had kept tabs on him. They might have found him a safe haven, given him a new identity and a job, protected him from those in the Agency who would never forgive what he had done. But they wouldn't have cut the strings.

"Obviously I don't know all I should know about her. She didn't want to talk, at least not yet, and I didn't want to push it. Maybe I should have. But she's in trouble now, she's running from I don't know who or what, and I have to find her."

Thornton said nothing, and that brought a prickling to the back of McLean's neck. And, an instant later, anger. "You goddamned sons of bitches, you *know!*"

"Take it easy, Barney. You don't think they'd let you move in with someone without checking on her, do you? They'd have to do that."

McLean's voice was cold, flat, without friendliness for the first time. "I have to find her. Where would she run?"

"You can't do that, Barney! Maybe your cover's broken now, I'm not sure. But Zeller's doing his best to pull some strings out there in California and get what's happened under wraps as much as possible. We might be able to contain it. But we can't have you thrashing around. Go to ground, Barney. Stay put. As soon as it's safe—"

"No go, Paul. How much do you know about Angie? I need everything."

Thornton hesitated, but as it turned out he wasn't wrestling with his conscience. "That's just it. We don't know much of anything."

"What the hell are you talking about, Paul? You said Zeller checked on her."

"She . . . she's protected, Barney. She's in the witness program. It . . . it's just a coincidence, that's all, a freak thing that you'd get together with someone like that. It wouldn't happen again in a million years . . ."

His voice faded as understanding flooded McLean's brain. "God almighty," he whispered.

"What's that, Barney?"

"It's no coincidence at all," McLean said. "It had to happen sooner or later."

"You're not making sense . . ."

"It's obvious, Paul. Two different government agencies consulting the same computer, or even different computers programmed with the same information and linked to the same data banks, each looking for a safe place to stash someone, asking the same questions, setting the same parameters." He laughed harshly. "Why wouldn't it happen? That possibility should be factored in there, too."

"Well, I suppose," Thornton faltered. That was one reason he had never been a good field man, McLean thought. The unexpected threw him. He could never hit a curve. The trouble with always being careful was, it didn't prepare you for the one misstep, the moment of weakness, the lurch of fate. "The point is, we can't get at her background any more than anyone else can."

"You underestimate Zeller, Paul."

"I'm telling you the truth, Barney. We asked, and the answer came back loud and clear. Her identity is protected, no exceptions."

"I need to talk to Zeller."

"Barney, listen to me! You've got to go to ground. I'll do what I can about the woman—Angie—but you've got to stay out of it. If you go hunting, shaking the trees the way you always did to see what falls out, word will get around. You know what I'm talking about. You won't be safe. You're still a target, Barney. There are people who still blame you for what happened."

McLean checked the clock above one of the computer banks showing arrival and departure times. "No time, Paul, I have to go. I want Zeller. It's almost oh-eight hundred. I'll call back at twelve hundred hours Pacific time. Have him there for me."

"You can't become active, Barney! That was part of the agreement. No more crusades."

"This isn't a crusade. This is personal."

"It's always personal with you. They'll never believe you. A lot of them didn't believe you three years ago, and they won't now."

"Twelve hundred hours, Paul. And tell Zeller I want to know who she is. I have to know where *she* would go to ground."

He hung up on Paul Thornton's anguished protests and hurried toward the PSA departure gate.

4

THE United 727 TOOK A LONG TIME gathering itself together as it rumbled down the runway. When it finally heaved off the ground it climbed steeply through the thick cloud layer. For some moments McLean in his window seat saw only the gray fog whirling past the window. It matched his mood. Then the aircraft burst through the clouds into bright morning sunshine. McLean felt no answering lift of spirit.

Tony was nearly three now. Old enough to be confused and scared. McLean wondered where Angie was taking the boy, and if she was simply running out of control or acting out a preconceived plan of flight. He opted for the latter. She would have had that plan hidden away, just as he had had his own escape kit hidden under its false panel in the toolbox in the garage.

McLean felt no sense of betrayal. Tony's life meant more to Angie than her own. He knew that much about her for certain.

More than McLean's life, too, and he could accept that. She had probably convinced herself—or tried to—that anyone who came looking for her and Tony and found them missing would try to pick up the scent but would leave McLean alone. After all, he was nothing to them. He should have nothing to fear.

Even if she didn't really believe that, she would have had to do what she did. The only viable alternative would have been to tell McLean everything, and either she couldn't do that or she wasn't ready to.

They were a pair, McLean thought. Mystery guests in each other's bed.

There was a *ping*! and the No Smoking sign went off. Out of old habit McLean's hand started to reach for his shirt pocket. He had given up smoking eighteen months ago at Angie's insistence. She didn't like the way cigarette smoke clung to everything in the house, she said—draperies, furniture, clothing. The real reason she wanted him to give up the habit, he believed, was because his second pack of the day invariably started him coughing.

He tilted his seat back and stared out of the window at the unbroken blue. The captain's voice floated reassuringly through the cabin. Altitude such-and-such, clear in Los Angeles this morning, hot, expected temperature of eighty-six degrees Fahrenheit. The slight delay in departure would be made up en route and the United flight would arrive on time at LAX. And thank you for flying . . . fill in blank.

Lots of blanks to be filled in, McLean thought, shaking his head at a tired-eyed flight attendant's offer of coffee or something else to drink. Start with the phone call. Someone had warned Angie. A friend, a relative. But that meant that Angie had made a common mistake, falling into the trap of letting someone know—someone she was sure she could trust—where she was and how to reach her. Either way was a prescription for disaster.

All it took to undercut the whole program was one small slip. A tapped phone, an intercepted letter, a chance remark, an expression of joy where there should have been none . . .

The expertise developed for the government's Witness Protection Program had served a variety of purposes. Essentially the idea was to create a completely new identity for someone whose life might otherwise be threatened, and whose service to the country—usually testimony in a significant government prosecution—justified the considerable expense of such extraordinary measures.

The first purpose of the program had been to protect witnesses in organized crime cases. The Mob's arm was as long as its memory, and intimidation or elimination of damaging witnesses was standard procedure. Starting with Bobby Kennedy's efforts as attorney general of the United States, the Justice Department had had a difficult time convicting known organized crime figures of anything other than bookkeeping lapses. Witnesses in capital crime cases had a way of disappearing, changing their testimony, or suddenly becoming forgetful when they were put on the stand. When you found witnesses who were willing to take the real risk involved in testifying but who feared reprisals against themselves or members of their families, the Witness Protection Program offered a solution. An extreme one, but maybe the only one. It had created a new bureaucracy dedicated to keeping witnesses alive—stashing them somewhere out of reach until their testimony could be given, and then creating a new life for them afterwards.

It hadn't always worked. McLean remembered a well-publicized case—there had even been a movie—in which a husband and father had been denied knowledge of the whereabouts and new identities of his ex-wife and their children. As far as the government was concerned, he had no right to know. The witness—the woman in the case—and her children were the government's sole responsibility. Letting the ex know where they were was as dangerous as taking out an ad in the newspaper.

Sometimes people simply were unable to cut off all ties. The psychological burden became too heavy. They wrote letters and thought they were clever in mailing them from another town, say twenty miles away. They made long-distance phone calls. They went back to familiar places—a high school, an old neighborhood, a honeymoon site. They repeated patterns of activity—a star softball player looked for a new team in his new town, a woman who had been into basketmaking saw no danger in taking up her hobby with new friends, a Catholic child with a reading disability was enrolled in special reading classes at a parochial school in his new environment. Traceable patterns.

It was hard to make those who needed protection understand how total the break had to be . . . how completely they had to *become* someone else.

Witnesses who testified at great personal risk in government cases were not the only ones who sometimes needed the same kind of protection possible only by relinquishing their identities and, insofar as their old lives were concerned, ceasing to exist. Defectors were another common example. A new life in the chosen country, often a substantial income, placement where they would not reasonably be detected, a comfortable place to live—these were standard offerings placed on the table for an agent coming over from the other side with information valuable enough to bargain with.

Then there were isolated cases like McLean's. Someone who had to be protected from his own side.

Angie's placement in the Witness Protection Program explained so much. Her silences, the attempt to shut off all questions about her past life, including her marriage. Nervous tics, like jumping when McLean came into a room unexpectedly, or studying someone overlong who had seemed to glance at her with more than passing interest, or asking McLean if he had noticed that man in the gray jacket or the fellow in the blue Mustang that seemed to be following them. But even more than these things, Angie's role as an endangered witness explained her refusal to look ahead as well as behind her. She hadn't trusted the future.

And she had been right.

They were a pair. Each of them lying awake in the small hours, staring at the ceiling, not daring to look at the other for fear he or she might also be awake. Locked inside the cocoons of their pasts.

More than one poet had mourned the fact that the human condition was always to be alone, that all touching was illusory. That even lovers remained trapped forever inside their own isolated identities.

Even false identities, McLean thought wryly.

McLean felt the angle of the aircraft's flight change as it went into the long glide toward Los Angeles. Hardly time to get up before it began to come down. Hardly time for the harried flight attendants to scurry up and down the aisles, gathering up the coffee and soft drink cups.

The United flight dropped out of the blue into the yellow layer of smog that overhung the sprawling City of the Angels. During the descent McLean thought suddenly about the husband who had beaten Angie, leaving his mark long after the surface wounds had healed. He was part of her past but presumably not part of the problem. There was no witness program for divorce cases, McLean mused, even though having one might have been a good idea in some circumstances.

Angie was running from bigger trouble.

She was running for her life—and Tony's.

* * *

McLean drove south along the 105, the San Diego Freeway, through the bedroom communities of Westminster, Huntington Beach, Fountain Valley, and Costa Mesa into the heart of Orange County. Darkest Orange County, one agent had called it back in the Nixon years, when the president, who had regarded the Agency as a bastion of the "liberal Eastern Establishment" that had always been against him, had had his Western White House here. The land was flat and featureless. As he diverted onto the 73 Freeway toward the coast, he cruised past the skeletons of countless new office buildings rising everywhere amidst the clusters of condominium and townhouse developments. Exiting the freeway at Jamboree Road, he followed its winding passage through sculptured hills toward the ocean.

Off to his right he had a glimpse of the bird sanctuary and, defined by the distant bluffs, the sheltered blue of Upper Newport Bay. As he drove toward the ocean the homes became larger, more opulent. The day had been murky during the drive, a pall of heat and smog over the city, but here in Newport Beach the air was cleaner, the breezes cooler, the sky a dazzling blue. To the left of the road the rolling hills and canyons of the Big Canyon Country Club beckoned those who could afford the stiff price of admission. Here everything seemed new, from the sleek modern office buildings etched against the skyline to the sprawling estates overlooking the greens and fairways of the country club.

Topping a rise, McLean saw the Pacific Ocean, blue and sparkling in the sun, dotted with sprightly sails in the distance. He felt like stopping—"silent, upon a peak"—to drink in the beauty of the scene.

Instead he turned left onto a side road toward Fashion Island, the elegant shopping mall that was open to the ocean breezes.

The financial center of Orange County encircled the shopping center. It was just eleven o'clock when McLean parked beside a savings-and-loan office, one of many modern structures, this one of dark rose granite slabs containing sheets of tinted glass.

For the past ten years McLean had kept an account open here, just large enough to justify a free safety deposit box and dating back to a time he had spent several weeks on a stakeout of a yacht moored at the Newport Harbor Yacht Club, a yacht that had also been sighted in the harbors at Nice and Beirut and Majorca. Normally such an extended surveillance was about as boring as any law enforcement activity could be, but that was one time McLean had been sorry to have the stakeout end when the yacht sailed away.

Ten minutes later he emerged from the savings-and-loan office once more into the sunshine, squinting into the brightness that was always intensified by the glittering expanse of ocean on a sunny day. He had an additional three thousand dollars in two envelopes stuffed into his jacket pockets. He was also now wearing a leather shoulder holster that held a Colt Cobra .357 Magnum.

Checking the time, McLean saw that he had a margin before he had to make his phone call. He used a half-hour of it strolling among the cool, well-dressed shoppers in Fashion Island, past the gay umbrellas over their tables, the colorful flags and refreshing fountains. None of the shoppers appeared to be leading lives of quiet desperation. At a luggage shop he purchased a soft-sided brown suitcase, at the Caswell-Massey shop a toothbrush and comb, at Brooks Brothers a couple of shirts, some underwear and socks, a tie and a lightweight sports jacket.

Back in the rented Mustang he removed holster and pistol, zipped them inside his canvas carryall, and stuffed the shapeless bag along with his new purchases into the brown suitcase, which he locked. He had chosen the suitcase partly because it had a combination lock. He was always losing the tiny keys that came with luggage.

He drove away from the ocean along MacArthur Boulevard. A few minutes later, spotting the John Wayne Airport, he made his decision to stop. He had always favored airports or train stations when making phone calls under questionable circumstances. Such locations compounded the problems facing any pursuer who had to figure out which way his quarry would jump. He fought his way through the congestion in front of the terminal and swung into the short-term parking garage at the west end.

Most of the open telephone boxes in the baggage area were occupied. None offered any opportunity for privacy. McLean walked on through to the modern new terminal, past the larger-than-life bronze statue of John Wayne in a glass wing that dominated the front of the building. A wide-eyed ten-year-old had climbed up onto the pedestal to measure himself against his hero. All of the available phone slots in the lobby were elbow to elbow and busy.

Then McLean spotted a couple of wall-hung phone cubicles across the roadway in front of the terminal, next to a pedestrian stairway structure at the edge of the open parking lot. No one was near them to listen in.

He sprinted across the road through an opening in the flow of traffic. It was 1200 hours when he punched in a number and heard the phone ring at Langley, Virginia.

"How are you, Barney?" Eric Zeller asked, his tone as cool and detached as ever, as if McLean had been away on a short vacation instead of having been compelled to leave the agency three years ago under a cloud.

"Fine," McLean said. Observe the amenities. He needed Zeller's help.

"That was quite a show you put on last night. You shouldn't have done it, you know."

"I wasn't offered a choice," McLean said dryly.

Zeller was silent a moment. "We don't have identities yet on the two men you killed. Did you know them?"

"No. They were . . . another kind of soldier. Professional muscle, very confident."

"I see. A bit misplaced, it seems. That confidence, I mean."

McLean said nothing.

"I don't know exactly what you expect me to do, Barney, now the shit has hit the fan. Clean up after you, I suppose."

"That's up to you. Maybe you'd like the whole story to come out in the *Washington Post*."

"I don't like the sound of that."

"Neither do I, but I don't control that part of it." You can, McLean thought, and you will. Because it's in your own best interest. "I need information, and you can get it for me."

"I won't be a party to any vendetta, Barney." Zeller had become even more remote. "That's not part of the bargain. I'm not even sure I can protect you now."

"It's simple enough," McLean said. "You help me find the woman and the boy and we go off into the sunset. I'll never bother you again."

"Life is never that simple, you know that. You've stirred something up."

"It'll settle down."

Zeller offered him another long pause. The effective use of silence was one of the interrogator's skills, and Zeller had once been a skilled interrogator. "And if it doesn't?"

"It will."

The silence became different, acquiring an edge. McLean took advantage of it to glance around. An arriving plane had discharged its full load and the baggage claim area was a mass of people all appearing lost. No one was paying attention to McLean. Zeller said, "I can't take that chance."

"You'll have to."

"Oh, really?" At times Zeller could sound like a pompous ass, McLean thought. More than one adversary had made the mistake of thinking that was all there was to him.

"Don't hang up, Zeller," McLean said quickly. "I wouldn't advise it."

"Oh? Is that another threat, Barney? You don't seem to understand. You're not in a position to make demands or threats. You're out of it. For you, it's over."

"No. I took some precautions." This time it was McLean who let the silence hang there, acquiring substance, dimension, value.

Zeller's voice became twenty degrees colder, more openly dangerous. "What precautions?"

McLean smiled thinly. Zeller had not hung up. "The right ones. Anything happens to me and I don't check in every six months, my memoirs get published. You're in them yourself, Zeller. Not the star, maybe, but a choice role."

"No publisher would risk it. Not today." The CIA under Director William Casey, with President Reagan's support, had employed the threat of criminal prosecution to intimidate anyone publishing classified material. The campaign had had a chilling effect on publishers.

"Not in this country, maybe." McLean let Zeller think that over. In truth the London publishers who had read McLean's manuscript—he had met the chief editor by chance and liked him—were eager to publish, though they had continued to respect the agreement made with McLean that the final decision to publish remained his, barring his violent demise. Great Britain had taken so much flak from the U.S. over their embarrassing defections and other intelligence blunders that many on Fleet Street and in Clement's Inn would love to get some of their own back against the Cousins.

"It's old news, McLean."

"Then you have nothing to worry about." Not old enough, McLean knew, for Zeller to brush the potential damage aside.

"All right," Zeller said stiffly. "I'll see what I can do to call off the dogs."

"Do that," McLean said. Zeller had never been a friend, but McLean was turning him into something else. No one manipulated Eric Zeller. And he was not the kind of enemy you wanted. "What have you learned about Angela Simmons?"

Zeller hesitated. "Very little, I'm afraid."

"Goddamn it, Zeller, I'm not playing games!"

"Take it easy," Zeller cut in. "The information is protected. Maybe I can get what you want, maybe not. At this point Justice is stonewalling. They've been burned in the past on a couple of witness cases, and they don't want it to happen again."

"And you've stepped on some toes over there, haven't you?" McLean suggested. "They're not going to bend over backwards to do you any favors."

"Be that as it may, I don't have much to offer you. I do have the sense that she was involved in a major organized crime case in the East involving some big names. Angela Simmons is not her name, of course."

McLean thought about this a minute, wondering how much faith he could place in Zeller's words. He could be trusted up to a point, he guessed, until Zeller figured out how he might counteract McLean's threat.

"You can find out something else for me," he said. "She got a phone call, about seven o'clock, night before last. It had to be long distance. I want to know where it came from and who placed it."

Zeller considered this. "I'll do what I can."

"No, don't try hard, just get the name and number," McLean said. "You can give it to Thornton. I'll call back . . . I'll call him at his home tonight. I don't know exactly when, before midnight if I can. Does he still have the same home number?"

"Yes." The reply was Zeller's grudging agreement, McLean realized. He would go that far. Then Zeller added, "There's something you have to know, McLean. I said I'd do what I could to call off the dogs and keep what happened out there in Fortune out of the supermarket rags. But there's no way the story won't get around in our circles, no matter how tightly we try to sew it up."

"What are you trying to say, Zeller?"

"I won't be able to call Coffey off."

McLean felt a chill. Hell of a reaction to have after all this time, he thought. The Agency always denied having the equivalent of the KGB's Executive Action Department, to which so-called "wet affairs" were assigned, but if such a function had existed at any time in the past, or still did, Clark Coffey would be the man. "He still doesn't know what really happened?"

There was a brief pause before Zeller said, "There's nothing to know."

"Yeah." McLean considered it. The cooperation Zeller had offered was probably the best he could hope for. More than he had expected when he asked Thornton to have his superior standing by. He said, "Okay, but if he comes after me, Coffey or anyone else, he's on his own."

There was the slightest hesitation. "He's on his own."

What McLean was asking for and Zeller was grudgingly giving him was agreement that he could defend himself against the Lone Rangers without having to take on the whole Agency. "You'd better hope he doesn't succeed," McLean said.

"Of course I hope he doesn't succeed," Zeller said testily. "The Agency doesn't need any O.K. Corral just now. That's why it would be better if you just let us arrange another safe harbor

for you. We'll do whatever we can for the woman and her child.
If there's anything we *can* do," he added.

"You're not listening, Zeller."

"On the contrary—"

"I told you . . . if anything violent happens to me, the story
is out. Period. It doesn't matter who does it, Coffey or a drunken
driver or God in His heaven visiting a tornado on me. I can't
stop that any more than you can call off Coffey."

"Damn you, McLean, you can't pull this shit—"

McLean hung up. As he tried to scoop up his unused change
he dropped a couple of coins. He bent to retrieve them. He
heard more than he saw the telephone box disintegrate as a soft-
nosed bullet smashed into it, making a relatively small entry
hole before it exploded the box's insides into a meaningless
spaghetti of colored wires as the bullet expanded.

He came out of his crouch on a run. He sprinted across the
roadway in front of the terminal, dodging a bus and cars that
swerved or braked in panic. Someone shouted angrily. McLean
flashed a glance over his shoulder toward the open parking lot
where the shot had come from. Someone was stalking him. A
hunter, waiting in the brush for his game to appear.

The doors to the terminal hissed open as he ducked inside,
but they didn't close fast enough to escape another bullet that
missed McLean and shattered glass. He spotted the olive green
pants and beige shirt of a burly security guard on the far side of
the lobby reacting to the noise, turning toward him.

The baggage area to his left was jammed with people waiting
for their luggage. McLean bulled his way through the crowd,
most of them unaware of the reason for the excitement in his
wake. Bolting through the doors to the short-term parking garage,
he saw another security guard racing away from him toward the
smashed telephone box, the original source of the commotion.

As he ran past the glass booths of the garage attendants,

curious faces turned toward him. Everything had happened so fast that McLean doubted anyone would be able to identify him or even say exactly what had happened. He reached his rented Mustang, the keys already in his hand. There were only a few cars parked nearby, and his shoulder and neck muscles were taut against the impact of another bullet, the one he would neither see nor hear.

The engine fired instantly. McLean raced toward the exit booths. He didn't slow down. Smashing through the flimsy wooden barrier, he caught a break in the traffic as he emerged from the garage. The frontage road ran west, then curved into a full loop that brought it back parallel to MacArthur Boulevard— and to the main parking lot in front of the terminal, where the sniper had been waiting for him. Would he have anticipated McLean's quick escape? His route out of the airport? Was he waiting just ahead?

Coffey had moved fast, he thought. He must have been in Southern California, or close enough to get here as soon as McLean did—or even before him.

Had Zeller tipped him off?

Or was Coffey carrying out Zeller's orders?

5

Sometimes you had to be lucky.

The noon-hour traffic backed up at the stoplight on MacArthur Boulevard by the airport was like floodwaters straining to burst through a dike. The light changed to red just before McLean reached the intersection in the Mustang. Accelerating, he ran the light, tires squealing as he took a hard left onto MacArthur. The flood overran the intersection behind him, blocking pursuit. And it was a long light sequence, McLean remembered gratefully.

He ducked onto the San Diego Freeway almost immediately, heading north, but even though he was sure he couldn't have been followed out of the airport he charted a roundabout route. He swung off the San Diego onto the 55 Freeway, which carried him northeast toward Santa Ana. There he waited until the last possible instant before cutting across two lanes of traffic onto the loop connecting with the Garden Grove Freeway going west.

No one repeated his reckless maneuver through the loop, and for the first time since the telephone box blew up he began to relax.

He took one hand off the wheel and studied it. It shook a little, he noted with disgust. But he had got away clean. Coffey— if indeed he had been the shooter—had either been delayed at the toll gate coming out of the main parking lot, or he had simply decided that he could not pursue McLean, guns blazing, once airport security had been alerted.

McLean had never heard the gunshots. A silenced weapon, he guessed.

Coffey had obviously followed him into the airport. The question was, how had the sniper got onto McLean so fast?

The Garden Grove Freeway carried him back to the San Diego heading north. The puzzle of Coffey's surprise attack stayed with McLean until he swung off the freeway at Lakewood Boulevard. A haze of smog still hung over the small Long Beach Airport. McLean turned onto the access road. He started to pull up in the open parking lot, changed his mind and drove into the covered garage. He left the car behind a pillar on the second level. He locked the keys in the car and walked toward the terminal carrying his brown suitcase. The rented Mustang would be spotted easily enough by anyone searching for it, but McLean was gambling that Coffey would be slow to get around to the Long Beach facility. That would come later, after he had become convinced that McLean didn't go back through LAX. Or go to ground in Los Angeles.

The Long Beach facility was like a small-town airport. No giant umbilical cords through which poured the line of passengers between aircraft and terminal. Here the parking was only a few steps from the small terminal, which had a 1950s ambiance. You bought a ticket at one of the uncrowded counters, walked out onto the tarmac, climbed portable steps that had been wheeled into place, and entered your plane.

McLean's luck held. He bought a standby ticket on America West for Chicago. He checked his suitcase through, the Colt Magnum inside, which meant that it did not have to clear the security X-rays. Thirty minutes later he was airborne.

This time he had used a credit card from his second set of false credentials. The first identity papers he had shown were now obsolete. Coffey had obviously tagged the rented Mustang. He could follow that lead back to the Hertz office at LAX and find out what name the car had been rented under. The passenger list for the America West flight recorded him as Dave Patterson of Los Angeles. McLean was fairly certain that the cover name was not known to anyone at the Agency. How long that would hold true he couldn't be sure.

"You from Chicago?"

The woman in the window seat next to him was black, McLean's age or older (hard to tell for sure), whose hair was an impossible shade of orange. Her eyes held a smile that matched the humorous curve of her mouth.

"No, I'm originally from Detroit. Los Angeles now."

She sniffed. "Detroit? Cold back there in the winter."

"Not like Chicago," McLean said with a smile.

"Well . . . Chicago's got a bit of cold and a bit of wind. Chicago's got a bit of everything, and that's the truth."

"Detroit's got the richest mayor."

She laughed outright. "Coleman? Ain't he the one, though! Now you take your mayor there in Los Angeles, that Tom Bradley? He's not like old Coleman. I mean, he's dull, you know? He's a *man*, I don't take that away from him, and I guess he's honest enough as mayors go, but where did he ever get off

thinkin' maybe he might run for president some day? He's about
as exciting as a wet dishrag, you know? Not like that Jesse
Jackson. Now *he* can stir up a crowd. He's a man you can listen
to . . ."

McLean held up his end of the conversation with an occasional
murmur while his thoughts strayed. He had come down from his
high, the shot of adrenaline that had sustained him after the
shooting at John Wayne Airport. Contemplating the frantic moments of a second narrow escape, coming less than twenty-four
hours after the shootout that had left two men dead outside his
cottage in Fortune, McLean was startled by one finding. He
hadn't known how much he missed the excitement and danger
of field work. He thought it must be like being a star athlete, a
football player, say, who has enjoyed the closeness of team play,
the give-and-take, the raucous humor, the intense highs and
lows of the games, then has it end for him all of a sudden, with
no chance to taper off or get ready for the end. You were one
play, one wrecked knee, away from your last game. How did
you come down from that?

He brought his thoughts back to Clark Coffey. Astonishing
that Coffey had been able to close in so quickly. McLean hadn't
been prepared for him so soon. Had Zeller tipped him off?
McLean didn't think so, although he couldn't discard the possibility entirely. What was it Zeller had said? *We don't need an
O.K. Corral right now*. Which made sense. Unless Coffey could
have pulled it off without leaving any trail back to the Agency,
leaving only a mystery behind . . .

How then had Coffey got onto him?

McLean was not surprised by anything Coffey did, least of all
the boldness of the attack at John Wayne Airport. A daring,
risk-taking, even brilliant covert-action agent, Coffey was also,
in McLean's prejudiced viewpoint, a psychopath. He'd first won
a name for himself in a CT unit in the Phoenix Program in

Vietnam, where his counterterror team's principal target had been the Ban-an-minh, the Vietcong's secret police, itself an assassination-terrorist-espionage unit. The problem was that Coffey *liked* killing. If he hadn't stumbled into the line of work he had found or wandered the world as a mercenary, he would surely have ended up in a cell one day, padded or otherwise. He had a grudge against the world. He hated people almost without exception.

The exception had been Carl Warner, the man McLean had betrayed.

His seat companion, whose name was Ella—"Same as Ella Fitzgerald, you know? There's some say I sing like her, too"— continued to divert him with cheerful conversation, and McLean let his mind play over the day's sequence of events, searching for a pattern or an explanation.

He had placed his first call to Paul Thornton at close to eight o'clock Pacific time. Eleven hundred hours as they read it in Virginia. Running for the plane after hanging up, he had caught the 8:12 United flight for Los Angeles, which took about an hour. He had lost no time waiting for luggage on arrival, and he had used a false Amex gold card at the Hertz counter for fast service. He had checked the clock in the auto rental office as he left. It had read 9:45.

At eleven o'clock McLean had been in the savings and loan office in Newport Beach, emptying his safety deposit box. He had killed a half-hour shopping before he fought the traffic along MacArthur Boulevard toward John Wayne Airport. He hadn't had time to do much more than park before placing his second call to Langley at exactly 1200 hours.

Beginning to end, a little over four hours between calls.

Coffey must have been in Los Angeles or some nearby city early that morning—certainly nowhere farther away than Phoenix. But how had he known where to look? He would hardly have set up a stakeout at LAX on the blind chance that McLean might pass through the particular terminal he chose to watch. That was far too wild a chance, even for Coffey.

In any event, McLean had checked his back trail automatically, both in the United arrival terminal and at the Hertz lot, to make sure he had not been burned. There had been no sign of Clark Coffey's broad-shouldered figure—hard to miss—nor had McLean spotted the same face in both places except for one man from the United flight who had left the Hertz lot in a Mercury Lynx several minutes before McLean drove away in his Mustang rental.

Traffic on Century Boulevard leaving the airport had been heavy. McLean had cut down Sepulveda to Imperial Highway, watching his rearview mirror when he turned left onto Imperial. Passing the litter of abandoned buildings awaiting demolition in advance of another freeway, he had kept up his vigilance. Retracing his route now in his mind, he was convinced that he had not been followed.

Coffey had been waiting for him in Newport Beach.

The moment he had heard that McLean was alive, in California and running, he must have headed straight for the beach, guessing that McLean would need to go there.

He had known about the safety deposit box.

"What you smilin' at?" Ella demanded.

"Just worked out a puzzle."

"You do puzzles in your head? You got to tell me about that. My ex, now there was a man who liked to do crossword puzzles. He'd work one of those out of the paper every day, even if he didn't work at anythin' else. And fast? You wouldn't believe how fast he was . . . 'less you spent some time in bed with him." She broke off in spontaneous laughter.

McLean laughed with her, relaxing, part of the puzzle solved. It was always better finding an answer, even if the answer was bad news. He had no idea how Coffey had learned about the safety deposit box—probably he would never know—but at least there was now a plausible explanation as to how he had been able to find McLean so quickly and make his move with such stunning aggressiveness.

Only luck had been against him, siding with McLean.

McLean was still left with the question of how Coffey had been informed so swiftly about the events in Fortune, which had occurred—incredibly—only about eighteen hours ago. There had been nothing about the killings in the morning papers McLean had scanned—either in the *San Francisco Examiner* or the *Los Angeles Times*. Since the killings were obviously sensational enough to merit front-page coverage, it was clear that Zeller had acted swiftly to contain the damage. Small-town police and sheriff's departments were generally more cooperative with government agencies in such matters than were the more independent and prickly big-city law enforcement chiefs.

All of which added up to only one conclusion: Clark Coffey had been tipped off by someone at the Agency.

"You're not listening to me," Ella protested.

"I'm guilty," McLean admitted.

"All men are guilty," she said with a smile. "But that doesn't mean you don't have to listen."

"I'm listening now," McLean said. "And what was that about putting on five pounds while you were visiting in Los Angeles?"

"Mom's cooking—you *were* listening. And at the wrong times."

They talked amiably for a while, fell silent during lunch, which as usual left McLean feeling sympathetic toward the lot of flight attendants—sky waitresses, he thought—and shared insights and skepticism about the in-flight movie, a comedy about an eager widow and a reluctant retired banker in Florida. About halfway through, the story did a turnabout and became the tale of an eager banker and a reluctant widow. McLean said he liked the first part best, while Ella enjoyed the last half hugely.

When they were circling above O'Hare at dusk, preparatory to landing, McLean gazed down at the greener pastures below, picking out the well-groomed fairways of a golf course streaked by rays of the setting sun. He broke a brief silence. "Ella, how'd you like to do me a favor?"

"Depends," she said cautiously. "After that movie . . ."

"Nothing like that. Just buy me a ticket from Chicago to Washington, D.C., nonstop. We can see what's available."

"You goin' to see the president?"

"Not this trip."

She laughed. "I like that. You said that as if you really meant it, like you were used to stopping in at the White House to say hello." Her dark eyes were shrewd, appraising. "You in some kind of trouble, honey?"

"Nothing you'd be ashamed of."

"That may not be saying a whole hell of a lot."

"I don't believe that," McLean said, meaning it. "Will you get the ticket for me?"

There was a pause, Ella's smile fading into thoughtfulness. Finally she said, "Assuming I was to buy this ticket, who shall I say it's for?"

"Why not for your ex?"

She was silent for a moment, continuing to study him. "That why you been playin' up to me?"

"I thought you were playing up to me."

She broke into one of her broad grins. "So I was, honey, so I was. I'll buy you a ticket in the name of my ex. I've still got his name on my driver's license, would you believe it? About the only thing that dude left me."

"Except for some good memories, I'd guess."

"A few of those. Yes, I do have a few of those . . ."

The plane began its run toward the strip of lights defining a runway, and the ground rushed toward them. When the wheels touched down gently, the passengers broke into a brief round of relieved applause.

6

WALKING INTO THE LION'S DEN might have seemed foolhardy at first glance, but McLean was convinced that no one would expect him in Washington so soon. Then again, he hadn't anticipated Coffey's ability to surface in Newport Beach less than twenty-four hours after he broke his cover.

Surveillance activity at Dulles International was routine, but it was directed at international, not domestic arrivals and departures.

There had been a wait of two hours at O'Hare for the next available flight to Washington, D.C., on United. With the late departure and another time-zone change, it was well after dark when McLean stepped from the plane above the wet tarmac at Dulles. In the moment between leaving the aircraft and entering the cumbersome shuttle bus that would carry him and his fellow passengers to the huge winged terminal, McLean felt the muggy night air caress his face like a warm hand.

Washington in May. Warm rain. Dogwood still in bloom in the parks and along the roadside. McLean felt a tug of nostalgia, like a fleeting glimpse of a lost love.

McLean had telephoned Paul Thornton at his home from O'Hare, and Thornton was waiting for him when he walked into the terminal. "Good to see you, Barney!" he said with convincing fervor, gripping McLean's hand. He glanced around nervously—like a comic spy in a movie, McLean thought—and said, "No luggage?"

"Just one suitcase."

Thornton gave him a sharp glance, the obvious question in his eyes—*Does that mean you're carrying?* McLean chose not to answer the question, which seemed to add to Thornton's nervous fidgeting during the seemingly interminable fifteen-minute wait before the new brown suitcase slid down the ramp at the baggage turntable and McLean claimed it.

"Let's get out of here," Thornton said quickly.

Paul Thornton looked more like a miniature wrestler than a spy. He was a short, stocky man with a large head, big lantern jaw, a forehead like a prow to hold his thick black eyebrows. His hair, McLean saw, was now uniformly gray. The barrel-chested body and big head on a thick neck conveyed an impression of physical power. In fact, Thornton was nonathletic and the mildest of men, a career spook who had never harmed anyone and would have been shocked at the suggestion. What he lacked in aggressiveness Thornton made up for in old-fashioned virtues: personal loyalty, devotion to his family, dedication to the Agency to which he had given his working life, and a mind that fastened on details like Velcro.

They drove in silence, McLean remaining silent even when they headed in the direction of Thornton's home. He lived in an unpretentious split level near Tyson's Corners, a Washington suburb, which meant that one was more likely to run into refugees from the nearby Puzzle Palace, the National Security Agency, than anyone from Langley. To McLean's relief his friend had no intention of taking him home. There might not be current surveillance for McLean at Dulles Airport, but it was far more likely to be in place at the home of McLean's best friend—perhaps his only remaining friend—in the Agency. Neighbors also had a tendency to notice visitors.

"New restaurant," Thornton explained when he parked the Ford Escort outside a seafood restaurant. "I can walk home."

"Why should you do that?"

"The car's for you."

McLean said nothing. He followed Thornton across the parking lot, the stocky body burrowing like a small plow through the fine rain, and into the restaurant, which was so air-conditioned that McLean shivered involuntarily, feeling the skin tighten across his cheeks.

They went into a large, dimly lit lounge rather than into the main dining room, and found a candlelit booth in a corner out of the way. Both ordered scotch, and McLean welcomed the warmth sliding down.

"You're looking good, Barney," Thornton said after a moment. "Maybe a little jet lag, you could use some sleep. But I guess things were working out okay, until . . ."

"Until yesterday."

"I still don't understand what's going on. Has anything else happened? I mean, since you talked to Zeller?"

"Coffey tried to kill me."

"Oh, Jesus!" Thornton spilled part of his drink. He covered his anxiety by trying to sponge some of the liquid from his open-collared shirt with the tiny napkin provided with his drink.

Stunned, McLean thought. Thornton, a clumsy actor, could

never have faked it. His confusion was genuine, and so was the dismay in his voice. "I told you to stay put, Barney, I warned you. Oh my God . . ."

McLean filled in the details of the attempted strike at John Wayne Airport in Orange County. Thornton downed the rest of his drink and stared into the empty glass. *You have to trust him,* McLean thought. *There isn't anyone else.* The murky avenues of betrayal and compromise, in which few people were what they seemed, made up part of the clandestine world he didn't miss. Thornton, a perennial administrative assistant, had never been a traveler along those streets.

"I can't believe he'd take such a chance," Thornton muttered. The black eyebrows lifted as he peered from under the crags. "Did you see him?"

McLean shook his head. "Who else could it be, Paul?"

Thornton started to reply and thought better of it. "I don't know," he said after a moment. "Coffey has a lot of friends . . ."

"And I don't."

Thornton shrugged.

"Do you think there are people in the Agency who still feel strongly enough that one of them might have tipped Coffey off as soon as there was perception of a link between me and what happened in Fortune?"

"Yeah. You have to remember, he's earned a lot of credit in the Agency, Barney, you know that. From the old days. Him and Warner both. When you took Warner on, it was like you attacked the whole Agency. You knew what you were getting into."

"I didn't have any choice."

Thornton was silent, and McLean wondered suddenly if his old friend had ever wondered about McLean's role in the events that brought Warner down. If so, such thoughts had never affected their friendship outwardly.

At the time there had been an active search within the Agency for a mole, and more than one loyal agent's career had been shot down in flames by unfounded rumors or allegations, many of them spinoffs from the ongoing debriefing of the Russian defector Golonov. The defector had provided so much solid, verified information that even his vague suggestions were given unprecedented credence. No substantiation was needed. A whisper was enough to discredit a career.

More than one agent-friend of Carl Warner's had hinted that McLean might be the mole, a KGB plant. Why not? What better way to harm the Agency than to cut down and discredit one of its best agents, a hero to most of the operations division? Nothing had ever been proved against Warner. Who really knew what happened?

Clark Coffey was one of those who regarded Warner as a hero, and McLean as a traitor . . .

"What do people in the Agency really think these days, Paul? What do *you* think?"

Thornton looked hurt. "I don't deserve that, Barney."

"Don't tell me you haven't had any misgivings."

Thornton flushed, glanced away, then covered his confusion by looking around for the waitress. "You want another?" he blurted.

"Yes."

Thornton waited until the waitress had left with their order. McLean glanced around. It was a pleasant room, he thought, with its cream-colored walls and colonial fixtures and discreet lighting. There was a piano off in one corner, dark and deserted although this was a busy Friday night. The room was quiet except for a subdued babble of conversation, the clink of glasses, and an undercurrent of sound from the color television set suspended over one end of the bar.

"Most people think that . . . that there must have been something. Where there's smoke and all that. At the time, the way most of them saw it, you were the villain of the piece. No one loves an internal spy anyway, and the perception was that that was your assignment. No one believed that Carl Warner could have gone dirty. He was too much an Agency man. But after a while most of us—including me—realized that there must have been something or you wouldn't have been sent after him." Thornton paused, treading awkward ground. "It was hard on his family, you know."

"He should have thought of that."

Thornton hunched over the table, his blue eyes sad over their pouches. "The thing is . . . I'm not asking you, Barney, I know you can't tell me what really happened . . . but no one ever believed in Warner's suicide. Especially Coffey. Warner just wasn't the type. They say Coffey went crazy for a while, Barney, trying to find you. Then he dropped out of sight, and I heard he was in Nicaragua, and then in Africa."

"Where is he now?"

Thornton looked uneasy. "I checked. He's been working out on the Coast and on the Mexican border. There was a travel voucher for Mexico City a few weeks ago, and back."

"Back to where?"

"San Diego."

Close enough, McLean thought, for him to make it to Newport Beach within the time frame.

The fresh drinks arrived and Thornton seized his with relief. "Someone could have tipped Coffey off from here last night or early this morning," he said after he'd gulped part of the scotch. "He obviously never knew where you were—no one did. But the flag notice came in from your insurance company contact around midnight. That would have been the tipoff. After all, we don't have many situations like yours. Someone who remembered you, and didn't like what you did or what he thought you did, might have put two and two together. That's our business, after all," he added with a rueful smile. "Adding things up."

"So it is," McLean murmured.

"It doesn't exactly take a quantum leap to figure out that the man we had under wraps out in Fortune, not a defector but someone connected with the Agency, might be the notorious Bernard McLean."

"And said someone put in a call to the Coast."

"It's just a scenario."

McLean smiled at his old friend. "Here's another one, Paul. Zeller could simply have called Coffey on the phone as soon as he heard from you what happened last night."

"I don't buy it for a minute, Barney. I know you two never got along, which is putting it mildly, but the Agency is everything to that man. He's fanatic about it. Besides, wasn't he part of the team that debriefed you?"

"Yes," McLean admitted.

"Then he *knows* what happened. He knows the truth. He's probably one of the few in the Agency who also knew where you were living these past three years. Why would he suddenly decide to tell Coffey?"

"Because all of a sudden I was a threat to his beloved Agency. I keep thinking about that, Paul. If protecting the Agency could best be achieved under new and different circumstances by eliminating the problem—namely me—Zeller wouldn't hesitate."

"But you warned him about that!"

"He told you?"

Thornton colored, the flush visible even in the pale light from the candle fixture above the booth. "He asked me if I knew anything about your 'memoirs.' Jesus, Barney, did you really write one of those damned hang-out-the-dirty-linen books?"

McLean did not answer the question directly. Instead he said,

"If someone—Zeller, for instance—gave Coffey the official green light, it would have been *before* I talked to him this afternoon. Before he knew there was a threat of disclosure."

Thornton leaned back and scrubbed his scalp with blunt fingers, thinking it over. "In that case . . . Zeller would call Coffey off now that he knows. He wouldn't have had time to stop the first attempted hit, since it came right after you hung up. But he'd stop it there."

"That's like trying to talk a runaway truck into slowing down." McLean shook his head irritably. "I'll just have to keep looking over my shoulder. Meanwhile . . . was Zeller able to learn anything about that long-distance phone call to my place the night before the shooting?"

Thornton nodded slowly. "Zeller put me on it, since I was already involved. He's playing this close to the vest, Barney. As few people as possible. Anything that comes in on you or the Fortune affair is for his eyes only. There was a long-distance call that night, at six-forty-three P.M. from Detroit. A public phone. It's my guess that it was a cut-out. That the original call would have been from someplace else."

"No way of tracing it back from that phone booth?"

"Not a chance. You're sure Detroit isn't where she would go?"

"Fairly sure."

The two men fell silent. McLean studied his friend's worried expression with affection. "Hell of a thing," Thornton said after a while, "coming home and finding your . . . your woman and the boy gone like that. I don't know what I'd do if I came home and Janie was gone, and a couple hoods from her past that I didn't know about jumped me."

"Maybe you'd do what I did."

"I doubt I could do it, Barney."

"Let's hope you never have to find out."

"Yeah."

"Does Zeller know you were meeting me tonight?"

"No, he only knew you'd call me. He didn't know you were coming here. If he had, I think he'd have wanted to meet you himself."

"I imagine he would have," McLean said dryly. "I think we've been together long enough for tonight," he added. "Thanks for everything, Paul."

"Take the car," Thornton said quickly. "Don't tell me what you're going to do, I'd just as soon not know if I'm asked. It's my son-in-law's car. Registered in his name, he just left it with me while he and Linda are in Europe, bumming around for two months."

"I'm sorry I missed the wedding."

"Linda was, too. The car should be safe, Barney, as long as you'll need it. No reason for it to show on any list connected to me."

"Zeller is very meticulous, if I remember. And Coffey even more so."

"I wouldn't suggest it if I didn't think it would be safe."

"I know that, and I'm grateful, Paul. But I don't want you to stick your neck out any more than you have. Give me till morning if you can. Then tell Zeller I was here and you met me. Tell him what we talked about." He paused. "Can you drive me to the nearest Metro station?"

"Sure, if that's what you want. Where are you going?"

McLean hesitated, fighting the sag of fatigue. It was late but he could still catch a flight out of Washington's National Airport for Philadelphia. "To find Angie," he said.

Philadelphia, he was thinking, was the one place he could definitely link to Angie's past.

7

THE FLIGHT OUT OF Washington's National Airport for Philadelphia International was short and uneventful. McLean had started to doze when the plane dropped out of midnight darkness toward the sprawl of the city, the gray wash of the Delaware River pale in the moonlight.

Ready to drop, McLean retrieved his suitcase from the baggage claim and grabbed a shuttle bus to the Quality Inn there at the airport. He didn't care where he stopped for the night as long as it was clean and close by.

For a few minutes, alone in the silent room, he stared out of the window toward the city. Foolish to believe that he could *feel* Angie out there somewhere, send telepathic antennae reaching out to her. And yet . . . he felt that she was here. In this city. This was where she would come.

There was a tendency to think of people running for remote places when they wanted to evade pursuit or hide. More often than not they would seek out familiar haunts, places where they knew all the nooks and crannies, the streets and alleys. Where they might have friends ready to help.

McLean lay on the bed without undressing, locking hands behind his neck and staring up at the ceiling, thinking that he would try to plumb his memory for clues.

When he awoke sunlight streamed through the window.

In the morning he bought toilet articles, including a package of plastic-handled razors, and a case to hold them. Two of the razors were needed to scrape off his full beard, leaving only a full mustache. Tom Selleck reborn, he thought wryly. The facial skin was pale, an unhealthy white, where the beard had been, and he covered the area with a self-tanning lotion until he was satisfied. *You'd look ten years younger if you shaved it off.* Different anyway, he hoped, regarding the stranger in the mirror.

He rented a Chevrolet Celebrity from Budget and drove into the city. Philadelphia's freeways, like those in most major metropolitan areas, always seemed to be in a state of construction or repair, and this morning was no exception, with one section of the 95 shut down to one lane and traffic crawling. Passing part of the construction area, McLean noted that few of the hardhat workers seemed to be doing much of anything. One of them saw McLean staring and tipped his hat.

McLean diverted onto the 76 and got off at South Street, close to the center of town. The streets were as narrow as he remembered them and even more crowded, funneling him past phalanxes of ancient brick row houses. It was garbage pickup day, adding to the litter and congestion along streets and sidewalks.

He fought his way over Twentieth Street and turned down Chestnut to Seventeenth, his goal, only to find that it was a one-

way street moving in the wrong direction. He had forgotten about
the downtown tangle of one-way streets. Twenty minutes later
he had completed a frustrating encirclement and was back on
Seventeenth Street. This time he was able to turn into an alley
that led him to the parking garage of the old Warwick Hotel.

The warehouse starkness of the garage and the spartan back
hallway leading into the hotel did not prepare a visitor for the
elegant intimacy of the small lobby with its slabs of marble and
glittering chandelier and huge sprays of fresh flowers.

After checking in and leaving his suitcase in his room,
McLean went out for a walk to get a feel of the city, which he
now thought of as Angie's city. In the days when he was on
assignment in strange places, the first thing he did was walk the
streets. Then, given the considered possibility of having to leave
in a hurry, he would not blunder upon one-way streets going the
wrong way.

Although it was a warm day, somewhere in the mid-seventies,
sunny and bright, along the sidewalks there was a sense of
briskness and purpose, of life in a hurry, that was missing out
on the laid-back West Coast. The difference, McLean thought,
was more apparent than real. He remembered someone in L.A.
saying, "Don't be fooled by all that laid-back stuff you hear.
You notice all those Mercedes and BMWs? Those are sharks
driving those cars. That's how they get 'em. This place is full of
sharks." In the East, McLean thought, the sharks just swam a
little faster.

He liked the little kiosks and sidewalk stands, though most
of them seemed to be selling the same fruits and pretzels, the
same inexpensive washed gold jewelry from Thailand. He liked
the way the women walked and dressed. He tried to picture
Angie growing up in Philadelphia, taking a bus with her school
class to Independence Square, ogling the crack in the Liberty

Bell and asking how it had gotten cracked, having lunch at Bookbinder's when she was a little more grown-up, trying out the intricate crevices of a lobster, learning to be cool and elegant at Bryn Mawr, shopping at Wanamaker's for everything from fashions to furniture because Wanamaker's was the kind of old-fashioned department store that made coming downtown worthwhile . . .

At noon McLean stopped at a crowded grill and ordered a Philly cheese steak sandwich. That Philadelphia tradition had lately become a California fad, available in many of the chain restaurants as a successor to the fading croissant sandwich. It tasted delicious, the slices of beef paper-thin, the onions grilled, the whole oozing with cheese and peppers. You had to eat the sandwich in a Philadelphia coffee shop, with the booths overcrowded, the cook in a bad mood and the waitress snarling at a complaining customer, to really appreciate it.

He spent the afternoon walking the streets, getting down as far as Independence Hall, whose ordered red brick serenity he could not help comparing with the gingerbread foolishness of the City Hall he had passed. He sat in the park watching a parade of youngsters just off a New York tour bus as they noisily lined up along with older visitors from the Midwest waiting to get into the historic hall.

He had been in Philadelphia a few times, doing the usual tourist things, but did not know the city well. Walking its streets, listening to its voices, soaking up its atmosphere, he had the feeling of drawing closer to Angie, in ways they had not permitted themselves to touch.

He had dinner at the venerable City Tavern, doing the tourist thing. Putty-colored walls with old nautical maps in frames, high ceilings, little flickering flame bulbs like candlelight, high-backed, green-painted Windsor chairs, white tablecloths, costumed waiters, the tinkle of a harpsichord from one of the front rooms. *Did you wonder, Angie, if Benjamin Franklin had supped at this table?*

His mood darkened with the end of the day as he walked back to his hotel, relearning Eastern aggressiveness as he coped with the light-jumping traffic. At the Warwick he showed his room key and was admitted to the club lounge, where he brooded over a scotch on the rocks.

He took the elevator to his room on the fifth floor, wondering as always as he went along the corridor why even the most discreetly luxurious hotels had hallways of bland indifference.

In his room he unpacked a few things, removed from their plastic and cardboard wrappings the shirts he had bought in Newport Beach, carried his new toiletries case into the bathroom. From the window of his room he looked down at the hassle and horns of Seventeenth Street in the early darkness of the evening.

He would not find Angie walking the streets aimlessly. If he was going to find her at all, he would have to do it the way he had tackled a hundred similar problems at the Agency. He would solve it by methodically going over the ground like a detective searching for the smallest clue, putting every scrap into a folder in his mind.

Angie had thought the notion of his having been a spy was a joke.

—*All I said was, I used to work for the government.*

—*I knew it! You were a spy!*

—*More like an accountant.*

—*Liar. You were a spy, no getting away from it . . . I like you as a spy.*

Although he had been recruited to the Agency out of Army Intelligence during the Vietnam War, and had put in an extended tour of covert action duty in Southeast Asia, most of the time working with the hill tribes in Laos against the Pathet Lao but including a harrowing six months operating in Vietnam behind the enemy lines or in areas that were Vietcong strongholds, McLean's strength had ultimately proved to be in something other than field work.

He was an analyst. And good at it.

What most people forgot, or never knew, about the Agency's role in Vietnam was that its analysts had strongly and consistently opposed the American commitment there. During its bad guy phase, at the time of the Church Committee hearings in the mid-1970s, flogging the Agency for some of its wilder errors had become a political and media sport. The result had left the Agency's role diminished, its employees—those who survived—demoralized, their effectiveness curtailed. More than three thousand employees were chopped from the payroll during the drastic cutbacks of those years. By the end of the seventies, the Agency was literally half the size it had been when the decade began. America's intelligence capability had suffered proportionately.

McLean had endured that traumatic period. Like many other professionals in the Agency, he felt some bitterness over the gleeful tendency to make it a whipping boy for reflecting or carrying out the wishes of the presidents it served. Pressure from the Kennedys—Jack as president and Bobby as attorney general—had led to the outlandish proposals to poison Castro's drinks. Pressure from Lyndon Johnson had forced the Agency to accept an operational role its analysts had almost unanimously opposed in Laos and Vietnam. Pressure from Richard Nixon had brought the taint of dirty tricks and domestic spying until Director Helms dug in his heels. And it was the Ronald Reagan administration that enthusiastically ordered the mining of the harbor in Nicaragua and condoned the Agency's disastrous Contragate involvement.

Through it all, analysis, rather than the flamboyant stunts and misguided coups, was the real strength of the Agency. What an analyst did, what McLean had done (and what had ironically brought about his premature retirement), was to take a score of field reports or a hundred photographs or a thousand random facts and search for the small detail that had inexplicably altered, the element that was out of place, the familiar object that, on closer examination, might prove to be something other than supposed. By analyzing a variety of events he attempted to make a meaningful projection of subsequent events that would follow logically.

It was not a particularly glamorous job, but like an archeologist's laborious and painstaking digging, chipping away at layers of history, it could be rewarding. It had its moments of exhilarating discovery, of savoring the pure joy of unearthing something no one else had seen.

Most of McLean's discoveries had been ordinary enough, usually confirming findings made by others, adding the support of concrete evidence and logic to patterns already familiar. Once he had stumbled upon something no one wanted to find, a discovery that, made public, might have succeeded in destroying an Agency only shakily emerging from its period of trauma. It had cost him his career, and almost his life . . .

Now, McLean thought, staring down from his window at the headlights illuminating the canyon below, he had to become the analyst not only of his own life over the past two years, but of Angie's. He had to sift the ordinary details of some seven hundred and thirty days panning for the glint of gold.

Somewhere in all those ordinary days, those casual conversations and random moments, Angela Simmons—was either her real name?—had revealed something of herself.

Good schooling tended to erase such things as pronounced accents just as it smoothed off rough edges. But not completely,

McLean thought. You couldn't grow up in New York or New Jersey—or Philadelphia—and lose that distinctive speech pattern completely. Angie was from the Eastern seaboard. Not New England, for there was nothing of the down-home nasal or the Boston "a" in her speech.

She had also had superior schooling, the kind of background you might imitate but could never really fake. Did that get him anywhere? Too many schools, McLean mused. Too many class yearbooks to go through without a name.

Angela who?

Clever that use of a cut-out for the warning phone call routed through Detroit. No way to know where the warning had originated. The technique was obvious enough to a former agent like McLean, but clever for someone with no experience in the clandestine world. Angie's idea? Or her friend's?

But he had known Angie's intelligence. He had lived with it for two years.

McLean lay on the bed in darkness, the only light from the window, a neon sign nearby on Seventeenth Street, the only sounds those of street traffic immediately below and, off in the distance, a siren like a scream in the night. He let his thoughts drift . . .

—*Somewhere you said Philadelphia. You told me that's where you came from, but I don't remember what it was you said.*

—*I didn't mean to tell you.*

—*You didn't mean to, but it slipped out somehow, and you tried to cover the slip. Did a good job too, because now I can't remember.*

—*I didn't want you to know. I didn't want you to follow me.*

—*But I am following you. I have to. Didn't you know that?*

Tony, he thought. Anthony. Did that reveal anything significant? Too common a name.

Her mother had been Greek. From the north, Angela said.

They had watched the movie *Eleni*, and Angie had been caught
up in the stark portrait of that environment. She had never been
there, she said. Her mother had died when she was three, her
father when she was fifteen.

No passport.

Ordinary days and nights in a seaside town out of the main-
stream. Reading in the evenings. She had worked in the library,
liked books, kept her job after moving in with McLean. Before,
when she was living in the Harrisons' garage apartment, Mildred
Harrison, an older woman with no children of her own, had
looked after Tony when Angie was at work. She had been disappointed to learn that Angie was moving out, delighted when
Angie decided to keep working and arranged to leave Tony with
Mildred while she was at the library, because McLean was also
away during the day.

—*Tony likes your beard.*

—*Tony just likes to pull on it.*

—*Same thing.*

—*I shaved it off.*

—*No more scratchy kisses? I think I'd like that.*

But Tony will miss it.

—*He won't mind. He knows one of the good guys when he sees*
one.

—*Is that so? . . . Yes, I suppose he does. I'm glad he likes you.*
He needs someone like you, someone he can look up to.

Someone like me, McLean thought. Someone with a beard to
tug on. Someone who doesn't beat his mother up . . .

In her reading she liked novels, mostly. Rarely any nonfiction.
No pattern there. A craving for mystery stories the way some
people craved sweets. But romances, too, and the occasional
serious novel. Liked Michener. *Chesapeake Bay* was her favorite
of his books. Because she had lived there? Knew the area?
McLean shook his head. It was all inconclusive.

She had never learned to cook when she was younger. She was delighted with the so-called gourmet frozen dinners. The absence of that particular skill suggested that she had not grown up in a home where it was taken for granted that a woman would have to know how to cook. Times changed, of course, and yesterday's taken-for-granted was today's surprise. Still, the fact became part of the mosaic . . .

He sat up in bed, jolted out of drowsiness, listening to another siren in the night.

That fire. When was it? Early summer. May or June. They had been in Oregon on a brief vacation. Stopping at isolated beaches to marvel at the glory of the surf, the endless stretches of sand without a footprint, black rocks in the surf and a sea lion barking. A picnic of smoked salmon purchased in a small town along the way.

They had stopped at Coos Bay that night. In their motel room McLean had turned on the TV set in time for the evening news. Tom Brokaw was narrating an anniversary piece on the disastrous Philadelphia fire ignited by overzealous police gunfire on a house under siege. The blaze swept out of control, a scene from hell. Two blocks of homes gutted, two blocks of treasures and memories seared and blackened and reduced to ashes.

Angie had watched in horror, visibly shaken by the spectacle. "They're always having fires there, the people in the ghetto, in the summer."

They're always having fires there.

She was from Philadelphia. It was the remark of someone who knew what she was watching. There had been shock, grief— and recognition.

"The people didn't start this one," he had said.

But she had recovered quickly, sensing error, and she had immediately started to talk about dinner, of perhaps going out and exploring the wild night life of Coos Bay.

—I didn't mean to tell you.

McLean had observed her reaction and noted her words, but he had not put it together. Afterward he had let the incident slip away. But of course he hadn't forgotten.

—An analyst never forgets.

—I was afraid you might have picked up on that.

—I tried to be so careful.

—You didn't have to be. You could have told me.

It was about three in the morning, waking suddenly after drifting in and out of sleep, that McLean thought suddenly: She was married in Philadelphia.

She grew up here, she went to good schools, she learned to walk like a model, she developed a fine clothes sense but never learned how to cook, she probably adored Grace Kelly. She became engaged to Mr. Right, who, after they were married, turned out to be Mr. Wrong.

But she was almost certainly married here, he thought. And the marriage would have been in the newspaper. If McLean was right, on the society pages of the *Philadelphia Inquirer.*

He lay back, and moments later was in a deep, dreamless sleep.

8

SUNDAY HE PROWLED STREETS that were empty even of Angie's elusive ghost. Monday began with coffee and a sticky bun at the crowded little coffee shop on Seventeenth Street across from the hotel. McLean arrived at the Inquirer building at ten o'clock, signed a security sheet in the lobby, and was directed by the guard to the morgue.

A buxom blonde receptionist interrupted a phone conversation briefly to point a lacquered red fingernail in the direction of another desk. There a potbellied, florid-faced man in his late fifties, with a fringe of long white hair that reminded McLean of portraits of Benjamin Franklin, brought him microfilms of the newspapers he requested, beginning with spring and summer five years ago. Tony was nearly three and a half. McLean was guessing that the boy would have been a fairly early product of the marriage, within the first year or so. Later, he reasoned, Angie would not have been as eager to bear a child.

"Looking for anything in particular?"

"A marriage," McLean said.

"You got a name? That would make it easier. I could look in the index."

"No. I'll have to hope there's a picture."

Ben Franklin raised a quizzical eyebrow, peering at McLean through intelligent blue eyes. He interrupted himself to watch the leisurely progress of the buxom receptionist across the room to some file cabinets. Then he grinned at McLean over his half-glasses, much as his namesake would have done, and left him to his research.

Two hours later, when Ben Franklin came back from lunch, McLean was still looking, scrolling through the filmed pages of yesterday's news, past forgotten crises, pennants won and lost, hijackings and drug busts, hurricanes and tornadoes, hundreds of Beirut bombings, acres of smiling brides.

"Haven't found it yet?"

McLean pulled a new page into focus and his breath caught. His reaction must have been obvious, for it drew the newsman over. "Marchetti Nuptials," he read aloud over McLean's shoulder. "I could've told you if you'd had the name, saved you a lot of eyestrain."

Angie had been a beautiful bride. They said all brides were beautiful, but with her long black hair against the white lace of gown and veil, her large eyes and aristocratic features photographically captured, she was breathtaking.

Her husband was handsome. A dark, curly-haired Italian, he resembled a young Victor Mature, with lips that might have been carved in marble, an aquiline nose, long-lashed dark eyes. Bride and groom were together in one photo, and he was a full head taller. A big man.

The bride, Angela Stevens, ward of Mrs. Anne Stevens of Bucks County, had been a graduate of Bryn Mawr. The groom,

Louis Marchetti of Philadelphia, was a graduate of the Harvard Business School. The couple planned to honeymoon on the French Riviera.

McLean studied Marchetti, trying to see past the handsome features, the confident gloss, the Harvard facade. What he saw was in Marchetti's eyes. The look of the tiger.

"A real sweetheart," the voice said over his shoulder. Ben Franklin smiled at McLean's expression. "Sorry, but I used to be a reporter. As they used to say in the movies, one look at you and I smelled a story." He nodded toward the microfilmed page in front of McLean. "That one was a helluva story."

"It was that big a wedding?"

"Uh-uh. The trial. When that sweet bird sang." The man's smile faded before McLean's stare. "Hey, no offense. Look, I'm Ralph Hamilton. You're interested in the Marchetti story, maybe I can help. I was still on the metro side then, I know quite a bit about it."

McLean let his irritation slide away. Stumbling upon a reporter who actually knew about Angela was almost too good to be true. "My name's Patterson—Dave Patterson. What can you tell me?"

Hamilton's attention strayed as the amply endowed receptionist strolled by, but after a moment he brought his gaze back to McLean. He had drooping eyelids that gave him a sleepy expression, but the blue eyes were anything but dull. "It's a long story, Mr. Patterson. I'm afraid I can't take the time right now, but I can give you some of the dates so you can read about it."

McLean didn't think Hamilton appeared to be all that busy, but he said, "Thanks, I'd appreciate that."

The lengthy trial had ended three years ago, only a short time before Angela Simmons appeared in Fortune, California, and took a job at the high school library. McLean spent an hour reading about the grand jury proceedings, the headlined indictment and the tedious process of hearings that culminated in a dramatic courtroom trial. He had copies made of a number of the feature articles covering the trial. Then he approached Ralph Hamilton at his desk. "I'd like to hear what you remember about the trial," he said. "You free after work?"

"I never refuse a drink."

"We could try dinner," McLean suggested.

Hamilton brightened. "As long as you're buying. . . . Where are you staying?"

"At the Warwick."

Hamilton had caught the slight hesitation, and his blue eyes glinted with an old reporter's interest. "I can always eat a steak," he said. "You know Arthur's on Walnut? It's not far from your hotel."

"Six o'clock?" McLean suggested.

"You got it, friend. At six."

Hamilton seemed in no hurry to get down to the story. McLean, schooled in patience, was content to wait. "What's a reporter doing in the morgue?" he asked over drinks in the glowing wood-paneled bar at Arthur's.

"You mean, am I over the hill or did I drink myself into oblivion? I did my best, as far as the drinking goes, but that isn't how. I was a staff writer for the *Inquirer*, a crime reporter for years, that's why I was so interested in that trial the Marchetti woman testified at. I got onto a good story later that same year, a society doctor who was murdered, and I was sure there was a book in it, a guaranteed best-seller. Well, I found a publisher that thought the same as I did. Nice advance, enough to carry me for a year while I wrote the book. Then I would sit back and count the royalties from the deck of my yacht." He shrugged with an indifference that was not matched by the pain in his eyes. "So I quit, walked out, and wrote the book. It bombed. I took another year, wrote another one, even more sure-fire, and every publisher in New York got the chance to turn it down. When I decided I'd better go back to being a reporter, I'd lost my place in line. I'd been an arrogant son of a bitch when I left the paper, and that didn't help. All of a sudden, when I wanted to go back to work, I was too old. I could've gone to some small-town paper, maybe even found an editorial desk, but . . ." He raised his glass in a kind of rueful salute and emptied it. "I'm divorced, but I've got kids and grandkids here in Philly. I wasn't eager to leave or go off to some Sun City on my retirement. The paper takes care of its own, they offered me a job as a proofreader or in the library. I took the morgue. I was happy to get it."

The steaks were prime beef, rare enough to suggest the chef hated to expose them to the grill, tender enough to cut with a fork. The service was discreetly attentive, meant to leave a customer with the feeling of pampered self-indulgence.

Ralph Hamilton, who was a cigarette smoker, lit up content-edly over coffee and accepted McLean's suggestion of a brandy. Then he got down to answering McLean's questions about the Angela Marchetti trial. "I call it that, because without her there wouldn't have been any trial. But Louis Marchetti, who really should have been nailed, walked."

"Tell me about it. What I didn't read in the papers."

Hamilton grinned. "There's always a lot that can't be printed. It starts with Old Tony. Tony Marchetti. He's connected, one of the Philly Mob families. Like most of the families, Old Tony's has gone respectable in recent years. The money goes into legitimate businesses more and more. Tony wanted his son Louis to stay out of the real family business. He was a bright kid, handsome as Hercules, played a little high school football, and the old man did some leaning where it mattered and got him into Harvard.

"From there it was like all the best fairy tales. Young Louis got his Harvard degree, went to work in Philadelphia for one of the big construction firms, perfectly legitimate, or at least imperfectly legitimate, and started moving in the best circles. So he meets this Main Line beauty and she doesn't have a chance, does she? Louis, you see, didn't just want Harvard and respectability. He wanted it all, right up to and including the girl from Bryn Mawr, and the entree to all the best that society has to offer in these parts. You follow me so far?"

McLean nodded.

Hamilton savored his brandy. "Only one trouble," he said. "Louis is a sleaze."

"The trial was about drugs," McLean said. "Was the Marchetti family heavily into drugs?"

"What family isn't these days? But you know how they operate, you can never get close to them. The police grab a shipment just in from Colombia, and the newspapers jump on it and say it has a street value of twenty million, and what is it? A grain of sand on the beach. It's what came in this week on Tuesday afternoon, that's all, one bundle. The truck drivers are scared aliens who don't know anything. The people who are behind it all, Old Tony and the others, aren't even visible."

"So how did Louis and his friends get into trouble?"

Hamilton grinned. He combed his long white fringe with his fingers. "You think I look like Ben Franklin?"

"A little," McLean admitted.

"I cultivate it. Did you know he had quite a reputation with the ladies?"

"I've heard that."

"I cultivate that too." He examined the bottom of his brandy snifter. "Another?"

McLean waited until two more brandies had been brought to the table. Then he said, "Tell me about Louis. What kind of a sleaze is he?"

"Let me put it this way," said Hamilton. "Old Tony, the father, has been up for maybe a half-dozen killings in his time, never convicted. He's run numbers and prostitution and gambling and extortion. And he's a prince of the realm compared to Louis.

"The funny thing is . . . Louis is still society. The girl got him into society, but when she ran away it didn't hurt him. And when the government's case against Louis collapsed, it made a kind of Main Line folk hero out of him. He was one of them, even if he'd got in on a pass; he was being persecuted, and he beat the system. Everyone ended up blaming her for turning against him. Same way they lined up for that Von Bulow guy."

"How did he get into trouble?"

"He went outside the family," Hamilton said. "Thought he was smart, and I guess he was up to a point. The old man, Old Tony, wanted his son clean, with his Main Line wife and his Ivy League connections and a new baby on the way. You know the story, the grandson would be president some day, or at least Senator Marchetti. Old Tony forgot that Ivy Leaguers like to stuff their noses, too. Louis had connections. He could supply them with whatever they wanted, all the dreams they could dream, all the highs they could climb.

"This went on for a while, but then Louis started to get bigger ideas about developing his sideline. I guess straight business can be boring, even Harvard Business School-type business, which can make old-time Mob activities look like tiddlywinks. But Louis was raised on all the old stories about going to the mattress, the Kiss of Death, and all that shit." Hamilton paused, twirled the amber liquid in its glass and sniffed it luxuriously. "Besides, we're not talking pocket money here."

"No . . ." McLean murmured encouragingly.

"We're talking megabucks. And it was a free-wheeling scene. Anybody with enough guts and cash and no conscience could make enough in one turnaround to have old Pierpont Morgan groaning in his grave. Louis probably figured he'd go in, make his pile, and get out without anyone noticing, especially not his old man. Or maybe he didn't really care if anyone noticed. Louis isn't what you'd call a shrinking violet." The bright blue eyes regarded McLean with shrewd speculation. "Women love him. He's beautiful, he can supply them with dreams, and he scares them."

McLean said nothing. He didn't want to think of the dreams Louis Marchetti had offered Angie, or of the ways he had scared her.

"It was his wife who tripped him up."

"Why?"

"Why did she do it?" Hamilton shrugged pudgy shoulders. "She's the only one who can answer that. But I could make a couple of educated guesses."

"Try them out on me."

Hamilton lit up again before he resumed. His stubby fingers were stained yellow. "She was a sweet young thing, if you can believe that in this day and age. Raised by her aunt after her parents both died. The aunt died of cancer the same year Angela disappeared. When she didn't show up at the funeral there were a lot of negative whispers. Louis was there, of course."

"Get to it," McLean said, for the first time betraying a trace of impatience.

"I'm getting there. This isn't a newspaper story I have to get it all in the first paragraph. It's all relevant, Patterson."

"Sorry. Go on."

"She had a brother, about five years older. All-American boy, blond, good-looking, star athlete, even went into the Peace Corps for a couple of years. You know how it is with those kids, other kids suck up to them, they've got a little grass, a little coke, hey, let's celebrate. The brother, Grady Stevens, the older brother Angela worshipped the way teenage girls will, was given something new at a party one night, maybe it was too pure for him or maybe it was laced with something bad. Whatever, he went into convulsions, and by the time they got him to a hospital he was dead." The reporter was no longer smiling. "I'm telling you this, just speculating, you understand, because I think it had something to do with what Angela Marchetti did."

"She hated the drug scene."

"You've got it. On top of that, I'd say the marriage was going sour. It was a mistake in the first place, and she was bound to grow up fast. So you've got a marriage going bad, and I think she was afraid that Louis was going to take the baby away from her. So she began looking for a way out, and Louis handed it to her.

"She went to the DEA with her story. She laid it all out for them. It seems that Louis was using their family vacations in Florida and the Caribbean to carry out his little sideline. At first she didn't know about it, but after her brother's death she started paying more attention. The DEA put some agents on it. They set up a couple of big buys and struck pay dirt. They had Louis Marchetti's pilot, his accomplices, his pipeline back to Colombia, the whole works. Everything except Louis himself.

"Angela Marchetti stuck her neck out and testified. The only trouble was, she wouldn't testify against her husband, and he wriggled free. Without her they didn't have enough on him. But they used her testimony to shut down his network, which I guess is what she really wanted. And she hurt him bad. With his old man, with the people in Colombia, with the Mob. As soon as the verdict was in, she disappeared."

There was a long silence. Around them glasses clinked and voices murmured, but the sounds seemed far away. McLean found himself thinking, *God, you had guts, taking it all on your own shoulders like that, daring them to do their worst.*

After what seemed a long time he said, "What happened to her?"

Hamilton stared at him. "I don't know what you're after, Patterson, but . . . this isn't official, mind you, but it's not really a secret that she's in the government's Witness Protection Program. No one knows where she is. She's safe, her and the boy, where Marchetti can't touch them."

McLean leaned back. "Not any more," he said.

9

Stacy barrett was not at home. Would he care to leave a message? McLean demurred. He would call back later. Was it possible to say when Mrs. Barrett would return home? The maid or secretary—her tone had the aloofness of borrowed importance—was sorry, but she really couldn't say when Mrs. Barrett would be available. At that point McLean relented. He told her that his name was David Patterson, that he was staying at the Warwick, and that he was anxious to get hold of Mrs. Barrett about a mutual friend. He gave the Warwick's phone and his room number.

Hanging up, he reflected that he would have to leave the Warwick soon. Too many people knew where David Patterson was staying.

For about forty-five minutes McLean worked off some of his nervous tension with strenuous push-ups, sit-ups with his legs locked under the bed, and arm lifts while suspended by his hands from the top of the bathroom door. There was still soreness in his kidney where the small hit man had punched him, but it eased as he loosened up. He finished his workout with his chest heaving but his heart drumming comfortably.

After that he finished going through the morning paper and studied a map he had picked up of the Philadelphia area, committing street names and directions to memory. He was reluctant to leave his room on the chance that Stacy Barrett might return his call. He was not completely convinced that she had been out when her phone was answered; she might simply not have been accepting calls from strangers. The Stacy Barretts of the world made their own social rules.

Her name had been given in the story of the Marchetti nuptials as the maid-of-honor. Ralph Hamilton had supplied the information that her maiden name was Randall, and that hers was an old-line Philadelphia family that could trace its roots back to the Revolution. Her husband, Roderick Barrett, was a distant cousin of the Barrett Hotels family. He was an investment counselor. No hotels, Hamilton had added with a grin. Too bad.

McLean had a light lunch sent up to his room—a chef's salad and some hot tea. He almost wished that he had ordered cigarettes but resisted the impulse. Angie would have been disappointed.

Over his second cup of tea he placed a call to Langley, dialing Paul Thornton's number direct. "It's me, Paul," he said when he recognized Thornton's voice.

"Barney! You okay? Where are you?"

"I'm fine, no problems." He paused. "Did you brief Zeller on our meeting?"

"Yeah. He was pissed off, but I don't suppose that surprises you."

"Anything new you can tell me?"

"We got names on those two gunfighters you tangled with out

in California. Both of them small time. One was out of Vegas, big guy, name of Raymond Ryder, alias Dutch Ryder, alias Harold Colby, alias Henry Starr. Couple of minor convictions, plus one felony extortion. He was inside for three years for that one. He was supposed to be a very hard guy, Barney. The other one, Benny Popolano, is from the East. Lately of Atlantic City. Same kind of sheet, except that Benny had a reputation as being very street smart. He was probably sent along to tell Raymond what to do." Thornton paused. "Zeller thinks you were lucky."

"So do I," McLean said. "Maybe I should talk to him. Is he available?"

"Let me put you on hold and I'll find him."

"No, I'll call back in five minutes."

"Hey, wait a minute, Barney, you don't think—"

"It isn't that I don't trust you, Paul, but let's face it, there's someone at your end who isn't my friend."

"Damn it, if they've got a tap on this phone—"

"Let's say I'm just being extra cautious, Paul. Five minutes, okay?"

He stared out of his window at a bright, sunny day. High of about seventy-five degrees, the weatherman had predicted, with increasing cloudiness in the late afternoon and evening, and a forty-percent chance of rain on Wednesday. Without Angie, who cared?

After five minutes he called Langley again, and this time Eric Zeller was waiting to take his call. "You still insist on doing things your way, don't you, Barney?"

"It isn't just a job this time," McLean answered, "it's my life. But that doesn't mean I can't use some help."

"I'll do what I can," Zeller said cautiously. "What is it you want?"

"I want you to set up a meet with Tony Marchetti."

There was a long silence. McLean wondered if anyone else

was listening in on the line. "How do you suppose I could do that?" Zeller asked finally.

"You don't seem too surprised."

"I know Marchetti's name. I don't know why you think I would be able to arrange a meeting with him."

McLean smiled at that. "Come off it, Zeller. If you don't have a connection that can put you in touch with Marchetti's people in Philadelphia, the Bureau does. Call in one of your chits over there."

"Is that where you are now, Barney? Philadelphia?"

"Where I am doesn't matter. Will you do it?"

"Where do you think this will get you, Barney?"

"Angela Simmons, real name Stevens, married Tony Marchetti's son. She also testified in a drug case. Louis Marchetti was in deep but he wasn't convicted, partly because they couldn't use his wife's testimony against him. But his coke pipeline was broken up. She made him look bad, upset his applecart. As I understand it, Louis is out of favor with his old man, with the other Philly families, and with some of the brokers down in Columbia. He'd blame her for that. That's why she was a protected witness."

"You're getting in over your head, Barney." McLean noticed that Zeller did not bother to deny knowledge of Angie's relationship to the Marchetti family. He wondered when Zeller had learned of it, and if he had intended giving McLean the information.

"You know what they say when you're in over your head, just move your arms and legs and keep swimming."

"It's hardly a facetious matter."

"I'm not laughing either. And I'm not getting much cooperation from your end. What about Coffey? Have you been able to pull him off me?"

"I'm afraid Coffey has been . . . incommunicado."

"Uh-huh."

"There's no point in adopting that attitude, McLean. I'll do what I can about Coffey. I told you I couldn't promise anything. I really think the best thing for you to do is lie low. If you won't let us put you in a safe house—"

"We tried that once," McLean said. "We also tried relocating me."

"It's not our fault you got yourself involved in something that caused you to break cover. That was your own doing, McLean."

He was right, of course, though McLean was not going to admit it aloud or apologize for it. "What about Marchetti?"

"It won't do, McLean. What you're asking could be very damaging if the media got hold of it—or if you got into trouble. We can't be involved with notorious organized crime figures like Tony Marchetti."

"It wouldn't be the first time," McLean said dryly. "Who knows, maybe you've even used Marchetti before."

"I won't dignify that with an answer," Zeller snapped.

McLean grinned at the phone, picturing Eric Zeller's frosty eyes, the thin mouth zipped tight, the lean ascetic features pinching in even more.

"Where can I reach you?" Zeller asked finally, McLean having waited him out.

"I'll call you."

"We can't help you if we don't know—"

"You can't hurt me either," McLean interrupted him.

He set the phone down gently on Zeller's protest.

It was four o'clock that afternoon when Stacy Barrett telephoned. She had a voice that was surprisingly warm and resonant, as if she had learned how to project it like an actress. But there was little genuine warmth toward McLean when, after the initial formalities, she asked, "Do I know you, Mr. Patterson?"

"No, I'm afraid not."

"You mentioned a mutual friend . . ."

"Angela Marchetti," he said.

"Angela? I . . . I don't believe I understand."

"You were maid-of-honor at her wedding five years ago."

"I'm perfectly aware of that, Mr. Patterson." No warmth at all. "But Angela . . . moved away about three years ago. I haven't seen her since, and I have no idea where she is."

"It's sad how people lose touch," McLean commiserated. "Mrs. Barrett, Angela has been living in California. A few days ago—last Thursday, to be exact—she ran away. I think she came to Philadelphia. And I think she would turn to someone she could trust."

"What is your interest in Angela, Mr. Patterson? I don't seem to recall . . ."

"It's not my real name."

"I see."

"I don't think you do, Mrs. Barrett. My real name is McLean. Barney McLean. That is . . . Angela knows me as Barney Redfern. We've been living together for the past two years."

"You seem to have quite a few names, Mr. . . . McLean, is it?" A trace of humor surfaced in the cultivated voice. "It must get confusing at times."

"It sounds worse than it is. Right now I'm in a little trouble of my own, but . . . that's not important. I'm calling you because I have to see Angie. We have to talk."

"Mr. Patterson—I'm sorry, Mr. McLean—if Angela ran away from you, that was her choice. It has nothing to do with me. And I don't really think it's my place to intrude."

"She didn't run from me, Mrs. Barrett, and I suspect you

know that. She was running from the same people she's been hiding from for the past three years, starting with her husband. He tracked her down somehow—probably because well-intentioned friends have been in communication with her. When she was warned that he had learned where she was, she panicked and ran. I think this is where she would come."

"I see." This time there was a long silence. "You seem to be very concerned, Mr. . . . McLean."

"Corny as it sounds, Angie is the best thing that's happened to me. No, make that the two best things. Angie and Tony."

"I see. I wish I could help you, but . . ."

"I think you know where she is, Mrs. Barrett. At least you know how to get word to her that I'm here and that I want to see her. I can help her."

"If she believed that," Stacy Barrett murmured, "she wouldn't have run away, I wouldn't think. Besides," she added, "how do I know you're not one of those people you say she's hiding from?"

McLean frowned, recognizing the woman's dilemma. "I'm at the Warwick Hotel, Mrs. Barrett. I'll be here at least through tonight, and if I have to move I'll let you know where I'll be. Angie knows my voice. Have her telephone me here. It's important. To me, and . . . to her as well, I think."

There was another long pause. "I'm not saying there's anything I can do, Mr. . . . McLean, but I will see what I can find out."

"Thanks, that's all—"

But the line had gone dead.

Unable to tolerate pacing his room like an animal in a cage, McLean went out for dinner. There was an Italian restaurant nearby, Fratelli's on Spruce Street, visible from his hotel window. He tried the pasta with shrimp in a rich sauce, regretting the garlic until he reminded himself that Angie was not waiting in his room. The house red wine made him appreciate the California wines he had grown accustomed to. He turned down the multi-layered Italian pastry in favor of a dish of ice cream. It was the first real meal he had eaten in two days, and walking back to the hotel he recognized that he felt better for it.

—*What did you eat today?*

—*I stopped at this little Italian restaurant.*

—*I can tell.*

—*That obvious, is it?*

—*If you get within ten feet of me, it is. For which there is a very simple solution.*

—*That's hardly fair.*

—*Life isn't fair. Neither is stopping at this quaint little Italian garlic restaurant.*

—*You're exaggerating.*

—*It would be impossible to exaggerate that much . . .*

McLean pictured Angie dissolving in giggles, unable to maintain her hauteur.

Stacy Barrett would have no difficulty keeping it up, McLean thought.

He wondered how the two had become close friends and how close they were. Did they grow up together? Both went to Bryn Mawr. Were they roommates there? Sorority sisters? How much could he count on Stacy? More importantly, how much could Angie count on her? The irony was that Stacy Barrett's protectiveness toward Angie might work against cooperation with McLean unless he could get past her suspicions.

A cagey woman, he thought. Sharp. Gives nothing away.

Stacy Barrett phoned again at nine that evening. McLean caught up the receiver after the first ring. "Hello?"

"Mr. Patterson?"

"That's right."

"This is Stacy Barrett," she said. He could hardly have mistaken that mellow voice. "Are you available tomorrow?"

"Of course."

"It may take the whole day."

"Whatever it takes, Mrs. Barrett."

"Good. You've arrived in Philadelphia during our Open House celebration. Have you heard of it?"

"No, I'm afraid I haven't," McLean said, mystified.

"It's something we do every year in May. I'm a member of the Friends of Independence National Historical Park. The annual tours are one of our chief fund-raising ventures for the park. We coordinate with other sponsors in arranging tours of many of the Philadelphia area's houses, gardens, and historic sites."

"Uh-huh . . ."

"You wonder what this has to do with you and Angela Marchetti?"

"A little."

"I have to be very careful, Mr. . . . McLean." Was there a hint of irony in the persistent hesitation before she spoke his name? McLean dismissed the question. She said, "I think you know Angela could be in very great danger. She might also lose her son. I will do anything I can to prevent that happening."

"So will I, Mrs. Barrett," McLean said quietly. Relief came with his recognition of the determination in Stacy Barrett's voice. She would be a formidable enemy, he thought, and a fierce friend.

"There's a tour tomorrow, by bus and boat, to Riverton. We consider it one of our historic places, even though it's on the other side of the river, in New Jersey, because it was founded in the nineteenth century by Philadelphians as a summer retreat. I've purchased a ticket in your name"—she interrupted herself with a light laugh—"as David Patterson, that is. The tour leaves Penn's Landing at nine-thirty in the morning. We hope to leave on time, so I don't have to tell you it's important not to be late."

"I won't be." McLean's thoughts raced, evaluating what Stacy Barrett was doing. Either Angie was in Riverton or she would be on the bus or boat with McLean. It didn't seem a bad arrangement under the circumstances, he thought. It offered a safe way for Stacy Barrett—and possibly Angie herself—to see him and make certain he was alone. Then either of them could pick the right moment to reveal herself. "Will I see you there, Mrs. Barrett?" he asked.

"Enjoy the tour, Mr. . . . McLean."

Stacy Barrett, he thought, had a way of cutting off conversation with authority when she was through.

Lying on the bed in darkness, McLean tried to rein in his jittery anticipation. Less than a week without her beside me, he thought, and I'm feeling like a schoolboy before his first prom night.

He wondered where she was at that moment, what she was thinking and feeling. Was she also alone tonight? With Tony? At least she had the boy with her.

He thought of something Stacy Barrett had said. *If Angela ran away from you, that was her choice.* But she hadn't had a choice, McLean argued with himself.

She had no family to turn to. She didn't believe she could involve McLean in her troubles. That had left friends. For Angie, McLean believed, that meant coming home.

Like her, McLean had lost both of his parents, his father to an early heart attack while McLean was overseas—for which he still illogically blamed himself—his mother to cancer not long afterward. His only brother Frank still lived in Michigan. Like many rival siblings, they had fought like cats and dogs as children, grown up into amiable closeness, and then gone their separate ways. Like so many families in the mobile society of the last half of the twentieth century, theirs had become fractured. The traditional support structure no longer existed.

McLean had never thought of going to his brother for help when he was in trouble. There was little Frank could do. In his adulthood McLean had found another support structure: the Agency. It was to the Agency he had instinctively turned the moment he was thrown into the open, on the run.

Angie had turned to her friends. From the sound of things, they were doing a good job of looking after her.

The impending reunion kept sleep away. Imagining the moment when they would meet, on the bus or boat, or after they reached their destination, he wondered if she felt the same eagerness. She would recognize him even at a distance. Would Tony be with her? McLean grinned as he pictured the boy's excited reaction. *He thinks you're one of the good guys.*

She hadn't married one of the good ones. When she came to McLean that first time, two weeks after their chance meeting at the high school football game, the emotional scars were visible. She had come trembling. Fearing getting into the cage with another tiger, he saw now. Questioning her judgment, hoping against hope that she was wrong . . . taking the chance . . .

—*Here, let me help you with that.*

—*I can take off my own clothes, fumble-fingers.*

—*Ah, but why should you? And why deny me the pleasure?*

—*Have I ever denied you anything?*

—*You've done a fairly good job of it for the past two weeks.*

—*Are you always in such a hurry?*

—*No . . . not always. Only since the first time I saw you.*

—*Oh. . . . Where did you get those scars?*

—*That was the last woman—ouch!*

—Let that be a lesson. Naked men should never lie.

—Is the boy with Mrs. Harrison?

—Yes . . .

—Good. We may be a while.

—Promises, promises . . .

—You're very beautiful.

—That's not . . . very original.

—The truth seldom is. Beautiful here . . . and here . . .

— . . . too small . . .

—No, no, just right. Perfect. And here . . .

—Too big . . . like . . . like you . . . too big . . .

—Are you all right?

—Isn't it a little late to be asking me that?

—I'm in love with you.

—I bet you say that . . . to all the girls . . . when you get them in this position.

—Say it!

—Oh . . . yes . . . I love you! . . .

—Uh-oh . . .

—Is it happening? . . . oh my . . . oh God . . . oh!

The risk she took, McLean thought, spoke more of her love than any words she might have uttered.

10

AFTER MISSING THE TURN onto Dock Street on his first pass, McLean found it and followed the narrow street until he spotted a crossing ahead with a stoplight. This brought him onto Delaware Avenue opposite Penn's Landing. The long parking lot facing the frontage road was to his left. He told the attendant he was with the Open House tour group, paid his parking fee, and locked the car.

He left his canvas carryall locked in the trunk. Inside the bag was his gun in its shoulder holster. Reluctant to leave the Colt behind in his hotel room, he had nevertheless decided that a crowded tour was not the occasion to carry a concealed weapon. It was too big and heavy to slip into a side coat pocket or to tuck comfortably against the small of his back. Probably upset the docents, he thought, if it drew anyone's attention.

The morning was cooler and overcast with a threat of rain. Most of the people waiting along dockside or near the tour bus wore or carried raincoats; a number also had umbrellas. Not possessing either, McLean was wearing his new Brooks Brothers blazer.

By the door of the waiting bus, whose motor idled quietly, a woman stood holding a clipboard. McLean joined the small group around her, waiting until he had a chance to give his name. "David Patterson," he said.

She glanced in a harried way at the top sheet, shook her head and murmured, "Oh dear, I don't find you." Then she brightened when she came upon his name at the bottom of the next sheet. "Here we are! You'll be with Tour A."

"Tour A?"

"Yes, yes. Listen, everybody! All of you with Tour A cards will be in the red group. You will go this morning to Riverton by boat, and come back this afternoon by bus. Tour B people are blue, and you will leave by bus this morning . . ."

McLean stepped away, absently attaching his Tour A card by its string to the top button of his jacket. The woman with the lists did not have Stacy Barrett's decisive voice. Several more tour members flocked around her, holding out their hands. McLean thought of birds in a nest waiting to be fed.

Where was Stacy Barrett?

He was disappointed but not surprised by Angie's absence. He had not expected to see her waiting in the open, among so many people. She would be on the boat, he hoped. Or waiting for him when he docked at Riverton . . .

"Does everyone know which tour they're on? We'll be leaving in a few minutes. Those of you in the blue group with the Tour B cards can board the bus now . . ."

McLean was one of the first to step onto the upper deck of the cruise craft. A steep central stairway led down to a covered lower deck. McLean went down for a quick glance around to verify that Angie was not there. Then he struggled back up the narrow steps while others were coming down. He stood by the rail on the starboard side toward the bow, directly opposite the small gangplank where passengers came aboard, with only the stairwell intervening. Here he was able to see everyone who stepped onto the boat.

There was the usual confusion, people changing seats, friends trying to get together, the ship rapidly filling up. Most of the tourists preferred the sheltered lower deck because of the threatening weather, which was the main topic of conversation. There seemed to be three or four women functioning as guides for the tour. McLean wondered if Stacy Barrett was one of them. She had managed to get him booked at the last minute . . .

Two of the guides were older women, blue-gray hair cut in short curls, sensible clothes and sturdy shoes, women too mature to have gone to school with Angie. Another, younger and pretty, wearing a tweed skirt and cashmere sweater with an expensive Burberry raincoat over her shoulders, had a winsome, pixie look and a fluttering smile. McLean ruled her out. Stacy Barrett, whatever else she might be, was not a pixie.

The fourth candidate was the only one McLean thought a real possibility. She was tall, trim, blonde, perhaps Angie's age or a little older. She wore gray pleated slacks and a white silk blouse under a blue sweater. There was something efficient and confident about the way she shepherded late tour members aboard, directed them toward seats, went about checking tour cards to make certain that everyone was with the right group. She smiled at McLean with casual interest, cool blue eyes quickly moving on. Stacy? If so, she was not yet ready to acknowledge him. He wished he had heard her speak more clearly.

A couple of husky young men took up the short gangplank and cast off the ropes. Moments later the boat headed out onto the Delaware River, which was gray and cold under the tumbling black clouds.

Out in the middle of the river the breeze was crisper, carrying a damp morning chill. The captain picked up a microphone after a short time and began to describe key points along both the Pennsylvania and New Jersey shores. Campbell's Soup off there to the right, just before passing under the Benjamin Franklin Bridge. A park over to the left, an historical site whose significance McLean did not catch. Another bridge ahead, named for Betsy Ross. The breeze picked up, gusts carrying a few stinging drops of rain, but the threatening downpour held off.

The guides passed among the passengers with baskets of large Pennsylvania Dutch pretzels and a choice of soft drinks. McLean stood against the rail toward the bow, munching his pretzel, unnoticed by his fellow passengers, listening to their cheerful, friendly talk without tuning in. Most of the tour members were middle-aged or older. Only a handful were younger than McLean, so he did not stand out. Some resembled eccentric bird-watchers in a British movie, but in general they were the mixed assortment of well-bred people you would encounter on any such tour, wearing their jackets with the leather elbow patches, their L. L. Bean shoes, their funny rainhats, their cashmeres and Irish knits, their auto-focus cameras on straps around their necks. McLean kept an eye out for the blonde woman in the blue sweater, but she stayed below.

Halfway up the river toward Riverton an elderly man in a bulky gray cardigan, round-shouldered and with thinning white hair, came along the rail to pause near the stern, a conspiratorial smile on his face. The slightly dotty uncle, McLean thought. He rolled open a brightly colored paper kite, checked his string and, with a wink at his fellow passengers, who were all watching him now with curious or indulgent smiles, released the kite. It rose quickly above the wake of the boat, snapping in the breeze as he played out his string, climbing higher and higher. The old man's smile became a broad grin of delight. Someone applauded. "Saw someone do this on a cruise once, and I've always wanted to do it!" McLean saw the tall blonde guide peering out of the stairwell, but her eyes did not meet his.

The kite, which was hauled in after fifteen minutes when the fun played out, proved to be the only eventful incident of the trip upriver. At close to eleven o'clock the boat moved in to the Jersey shore, docking in front of the wide landing of the Riverton Yacht Club, which, according to the captain's announcement, had been founded in 1865 and was the oldest on the Delaware. Also probably the most unusual, McLean thought, built on the pier in the form of an inverted U, allowing space, one of the guides pointed out, to drive a horse and buggy through when you were going to meet a ship. The clubhouse was on the upper level.

There was no sign of Angie.

Some of the tourists explored the clubhouse, others took snapshots, everyone milled around waiting to be told what to do. The guides passed out copies of the itinerary for the tour, listing the houses and buildings that were open, with a map of the small town of Riverton. The passengers from the boat, who had arrived ahead of those coming by bus, were divided into two groups. McLean's interest quickened when he found himself in the second of these groups, with the tall blonde woman as one of his guides.

Riverton was an inviting summer town, with its shady, tree-lined streets, broad lawns, and gracious homes. Several of the open houses for the tour were turn-of-the-century mansions facing the waterfront along Bank Avenue, large two- and three-story structures of dark, unattractive stone or warmer brick, their styles ranging from post-Victorian to Colonial Revival to an Italianate villa. These were the first stops of the morning's tour, and McLean trooped obediently along at the tag end of his group, entering the houses and shuffling through the rooms, eyes watchful, wondering when Stacy Barrett would make her move.

Angie was nowhere to be seen. McLean tried to put himself in Stacy Barrett's shoes as she had planned this rendezvous. She would have felt it safer to keep Angie out of sight until the last moment, perhaps when McLean could be cut away from the others on the tour. Sooner or later there would be some kind of signal.

"There'll be one more house," the guide announced as they came out of the Italianate mansion onto its wide veranda, "and then we'll have lunch at the Porch Club, where turn-of-the-century Riverton ladies first met to discuss literature and other things. But first, you mustn't miss the Borden house . . ."

Lizzie? McLean wondered, momentarily startled. But of course it wasn't that notorious house but a handsome white Victorian with porches and cupolas, stained glass and gingerbread, originally built by one Cyrus Borden in the 1880s.

McLean trailed through the house, falling behind most of the others in his group, becoming restive now. Why the long delay?

He emerged from a walnut-paneled library into the main hall of the house and spotted the tall blonde guide at the foot of a gracefully curving stairway, where she was talking to another woman who had her back to McLean. The stairway was roped off, the tour being confined to the rooms on the lower level. Two women from the tour came out of the dining room, in awe of the blue Chinese porcelain collection displayed in a large cabinet. They went past McLean with tentative smiles.

The woman at the foot of the stairs with her back to him turned to glance over her shoulder. Their eyes met and suddenly McLean was sure. Stacy Barrett! Even as he took a step forward she released the rope at the foot of the stairs and started up, not looking back.

McLean hurried after her up the curving staircase. A small commotion occurred behind him, and he looked back to see the blonde guide placing the rope across the foot of the stairs once more, shaking her head at another pair of tour members. "I'm sorry, the upstairs rooms are not open today. Have you seen the library? There's a wonderful collection of snuffboxes . . ."

Stacy Barrett had disappeared along the hallway on the second story. McLean had had only a quick glimpse or two of a young woman with trim hips encased in an expensive pair of cream-colored slacks, the apparently universal cashmere sweater, frosted blonde hair framing a strong face with wide cheekbones and a generous mouth. Striking violet eyes, McLean realized, matching the color of her sweater.

He moved along the balcony to the main hallway. The woman waited for him at the far end of the hall. As he started toward her she turned without a word and stepped through an open doorway.

Eagerly McLean followed her along the hall and through the door into a large, high-ceilinged bedroom whose lace curtains had been drawn over tall windows, effectively leaving the room in murky dimness on this dark morning. There was just enough light for him to see blue papered walls and white trim, along with old-fashioned heavy bedroom furniture that included a big four-poster bed to his left and a tall armoire against the wall on his right.

"Mr. . . . McLean?" The woman stood on the far side of the room by one of the curtained windows.

"Mrs. Barrett? Where's Angie?" He glanced quickly around the room, his earlier anticipation bleeding away as he saw that it was empty.

Stacy Barrett—there was no mistaking that voice—smiled and walked toward another door in the far corner. There she paused, giving him a glimpse over her shoulder of what appeared to be the tiled wall of a bathroom. "I'm afraid you've made a mistake, Mr. McLean."

"What do you mean? Look, Mrs. Barrett, I don't think all of this is really necessary. No one followed me—"

"Are you quite sure?"

McLean sensed them then, behind him. He stepped quickly into the room as he swung to face them. Alarm flared. "Wait a minute, Mrs. Barrett, *you're* making the mistake."

Two young men in T-shirts and jeans—college age, he judged, with faces still being formed—barred the doorway. They pushed into the room, causing him to fall back. One was a curly-haired, blue-eyed blond of about six feet who could have been a model for a statue titled Athlete, with his wide shoulders, trim waist, and every muscle sculpted. The other was huge, dark, and hairy, with arms like tree trunks, torso like a barrel, and no neck at all. He had jug ears, a nose that appeared to have been broken more than once, and the close-cropped haircut of a Marine recruit. Six inches taller and fifty pounds heavier than his companion, he filled the doorway all by himself. There was nothing mean or sadistic in the young faces, but something just as scary at that moment: a nervous determination.

McLean's gaze remained fixed on the baseball bats each of the youths carried in his right hand.

"I told you the truth on the phone," McLean said quietly to the woman. "My name is McLean. Barney McLean."

"And you're a friend of Angie's?"

"More than that. We were living together."

"That's all? Just . . . living together?"

"We're in love, Mrs. Barrett. Angie must have told you that much."

"Mm."

She still didn't believe him, McLean realized with a tug of panic. "I told you, she knew me as Barney Redfern."

"You lied to her?"

"We were both leading . . . secret lives. She couldn't use her real name, I couldn't use mine."

"Mm. And why do you want to see her now? If she didn't want to tell you where she was going . . ."

"She's in danger. She ran because she was scared. But you already know that."

"Yes . . ."

The two young men had remained silent, but McLean remained aware of them, aware of the youthful, steroid-aided muscles and the swinging bats. The bigger of the two was slapping his bat across the palm of his hand impatiently. Each slap had an uncomfortably meaty sound.

"Mrs. Barrett . . . all I'm asking you to do is deliver a message to Angie for me. Tell her I'm in Philadelphia. Tell her I want to see her."

Stacy Barrett nodded in the direction of the two young men. The closed the bedroom door behind them. It was a very thick, heavy wooden door, McLean noted, as solid as everything else in the old house. It would muffle sound completely. He could no longer hear voices from below or anything suggesting there were others in the house only a short distance away. He wondered if a shout could be heard . . .

The muscular young men pressed McLean back to the center of the room. There was no way out, he thought, unless he chose to attempt a dive through one of the second-story windows, gambling that he wouldn't become entangled in the curtains, or succeed in breaking through the glass and breaking his neck on the ground below. No way past the determined guards. No chance to reach Stacy Barrett before she could step into the bathroom directly behind her and slam the door. A connecting bath, McLean guessed, to an adjoining room, allowing her to close a door on what was about to happen and walk away.

"Oh shit," McLean said disgustedly, "you've got it all wrong."

"No, it's you who've made the mistake, Mr. . . . McLean, if that's your name. First in telephoning me and trying to use me to get to Angie. Louis Marchetti has tried this before. Angie is a very good and very dear friend. Even if I knew where she was, I wouldn't let anyone get to her through me, when she is, as you say, in danger."

"And the second mistake?"

"Pretending to be Barney Redfern."

"That's who I am, Mrs. Barrett. At least that's the name Angie knows me by. Why should that be a problem?"

"Because Redfern is dead," she said with cold anger. "Angie tried to go back to her house because of him. She saw the men on the porch who had come looking for her, and she heard the gunshots. She heard a man scream."

In spite of his own immediate danger, McLean felt an intense relief. Angie had come back! She had simply mistaken what happened in the darkness. Why wouldn't she? She would never have expected him to be capable of standing off two gunmen. And she knew he wouldn't keep a gun in the house . . .

Stacy Barrett might have read his thoughts. She said, "Redfern couldn't have fired those shots, Mr. McLean. He wouldn't have a gun in the house, because of Angie's child."

The contempt in the violet eyes was chilling. Stacy Barrett was a young woman who had known privilege all her life, McLean thought, who had never known insecurity or self-doubt. Beautiful, intelligent, well-educated, loved, and protected, she had acquired a self-assurance and confidence in the rightness of her judgments and actions that was unknown to most people. She was not accustomed to listening to voices of opposition.

In the silence McLean heard a gust of wind rattle the windowpanes. Raindrops scurried across the glass. The weather was about to spoil the Open House tour.

Stacy Barrett picked something from a shelf in the room behind her, and McLean felt a stab of relief. "A good idea, Mrs. Barrett. Take a snapshot to Angie. She'll know who I am."

"I intend to do just that," the woman answered, not trying to hide her disbelief.

She raised the Polaroid camera and aimed it at him. The flash went off in his eyes, momentarily blinding him in that dim room.

He sensed the two young athletes closing in. One of them circled behind him. The big man moved in front. "Damn it, Mrs. Barrett, call them off! Show Angie the picture—"

"Goodbye, Mr. . . . McLean."

The giant crowded him, black chest hair spilling from the neck of his T-shirt, a big man surprisingly quick and light on his feet, brandishing the baseball bat in one hand as if it were a baton. McLean sidestepped. But it was the curly-haired youth who struck first. He swung his bat with a rolling snap of his wrists like a real ballplayer, arms extended. The bat caught McLean broadside across his back.

The stunning blow drove the breath from his lungs. The pain in his back was unbelievable. Lights danced before his eyes. He stumbled to his knees. Through the flashing lights he had a last glimpse of Stacy Barrett's unrelenting gaze—hostile, merciless, offering no apology. Then she withdrew. She carried out her exit with consummate style, like an actress stepping off stage, quietly closing the door behind her.

She had lured him here, he thought through the red blur of his pain; she had set him up. Angie's friend? Or had he erred even more seriously? Could she be Louis Marchetti's friend instead?

He came off the floor in a rolling block aimed at the knees of the big man, trying to take him off balance before he had a chance to swing his bat. The giant used his free hand deftly, like an offensive lineman, holding McLean away while he clubbed down with his bat. It cracked off McLean's elbow, numbing his left arm.

From behind him the other athlete struck again. The bat glanced off McLean's shoulder and grazed his head. It nearly tore off his ear.

His brain whirling, McLean dove across the four-poster bed. He rolled from the mattress to his feet on the far side. The two young men stalked him.

"She has it all wrong," he said. "This is going to mean a lot of trouble." His voice sounded muffled, strange in his own ears. He was aware for the first time that his cheek was already swollen, his lower lip thickened and bloody. "Who are you guys anyway? Do you do this for a living?"

"We're friends," the big man rumbled, unsmiling.

"Angie's friends? Or Stacy's?"

"No more talking!" the curly-haired one said.

He circled to McLean's left, urgently beckoning his companion to move right, boxing their victim between them. The smaller youth gripped his bat at the end of the handle with both hands, waving it aggressively like a batter in the batter's box waiting for the next pitch.

McLean feinted toward the big man. He let the other commit himself, then spun around and stepped inside the vicious swing of the bat. He drove his fist into the blond youth's jaw. He sagged, stumbling back off balance, eyes glazing.

McLean wrenched the bat from his hands. He ducked and turned, but the punishment he had already taken made the pivot slower than it would otherwise have been. He had also underestimated the speed and agility of the big man.

The bat flicked in the huge hands. It smashed into McLean's side. He knew from the instant, crippling pain that one or more ribs had cracked. His legs wobbled and he could not evade the next blows as the big man flailed the bat back and forth, back and forth . . .

McLean's legs melted and he drained onto the floor.

He tried to cover his face and head, taking the repeated, brutal blows on arms, legs, a knee. The blond attacker had recovered enough to grab his bat and join in once more. For McLean the two young faces became a blur above him.

The young men didn't seem to be enjoying themselves, he thought dimly; their expressions were grim, even unhappy. They weren't sadistic killers but they were afraid he might be, and they were afraid to stop now that they had started. And he began to be afraid they wouldn't know enough to stop in time.

Another blow caught him flush on the side of his face. He fell into blessed oblivion, beyond pain, beyond fear, beyond the sense of loss as Angie's image fled from him like the last dwindling light of consciousness.

11

IT WAS LIKE WALKING IN on a movie you had seen before.
Waking in darkness. Feeling disoriented. Feeling battered. A
lip like a thick piece of sponge rubber. Jackhammers trying to
break through your skull. Had he only dreamed of it happening
twice? Or would he open his eyes again and find himself back
on his bed in the California cottage, listening to the alien laughter from the living room?

Face pressed against roughness. A rug. Nice Oriental rug,
though; pale blue background with pink and rose flowers. He
had noticed it when he first came into the room of the Victorian
house.

He rolled onto his back. Gasped as the pain burned in his
chest, stabbed at his shoulder, assaulted his head in waves.

He lay for a time with his eyes closed, letting the dizziness
spiral down. Couldn't stand the dark room wheeling around him
like that. Made him nauseous.

He became aware of sound effects in the background. Storm noises. Rolling crack of thunder. Hard rain beating against the windows. Dripping. Not a good night to be out.

When he tried to open his eyes one of them stayed shut. Swollen. With a careful hand he explored the puffiness.

The hand functioned. So did the other one, more or less. His left elbow was very painful but he couldn't be certain whether or not it was in serious trouble. Probably not, since he could bend his arm. *Just don't prop yourself up on it, son.*

Very slowly and carefully, fighting off the dizziness and the unsteady stomach, McLean managed to sit up and lean against the side of the four-poster bed.

The bed told him where he was, and it all came back in a rush. Those kids, desperately swinging their bats, as grim as missionaries. What had Stacy Barrett told them about him? Enough to make them believe that he was dangerous, some kind of a monster. And that he deserved the punishment he was getting.

Outside it was full dark. Old-fashioned shades had been pulled down over the windows behind the decorative lace curtains. On one side of the room the windows were black, their outlines barely discernible. On the back wall he could make out a hazy pencil line of yellow light around the window shade.

He crawled over to the back window.

It looked down on a deep back yard and garden with tall old trees guarding it. The street beyond, he remembered from the tour briefing, which ran parallel to Bank Avenue, was lined with old carriage houses, most of them converted into attractive homes. It was too dark to see much of anything below. There were no lights along this back street. Just one in the distance on the intersecting street. The light was made fuzzy by the rain on the window, and it seemed an odd amber color until he remembered that Riverton took pride in its display of turn-of-the-century gas street lamps.

No one would be out on such a night. Not even any cars moving along the streets. Nobody in Riverton was holding Open House tonight.

Going to the window had exhausted him, but he indulged the feeling by leaning against the wall only for a minute or two.

They might come back.

On your feet, boy. You can do better than that. A clown could do better. A second-rate movie actor playing a drunk would stand straighter.

Standing, he clung to the bedpost until the room stopped spinning around him. Then he dragged himself over to the hall door, that thick, solid wooden door. It was no surprise to find the door locked. He wasn't going to break it down, either.

Negotiating the interminable distance across the bedroom to the bathroom door in the corner required several minutes and left him weak, bathed in sweat. He tested the door handle. That door was also locked.

He wondered what Stacy Barrett had planned for him next. Murder? Was she up to that? Some people could never do it, regardless of the circumstances. He had a hunch that Stacy could.

Some friend. Angie was fortunate.

For some minutes McLean sat on the bed. The dizziness was definitely subsiding, but he wouldn't have bet against concussion. He probably also had a couple of cracked ribs, to judge from the stabbing pain each deep breath cost him. He also had more aches and bruises than he could count, so pervasive they all seemed to blend into one mass of distress.

But he would recover.

He didn't want them to find him when they came back. As

they certainly would. The locked doors said they planned to return.

He tried to picture the room as he had seen it earlier in the day. Was there any place to hide? Any way out other than the locked doors? Crawling under the bed didn't seem a very promising solution.

He stared at the ornate old armoire. Mahogany, he thought, with inlays in the doors. The piece was over six feet tall and almost as wide. Fetch a great price if they ever had garage sales in Riverton.

He went over to examine the big cabinet. There was a keyhole for a lock in the right-hand door, but the key was missing. He opened the doors and peered inside.

The floor of the armoire was raised, but a cautious examination revealed that there was no false bottom, no possibility of concealing a body.

The interior held a few musty articles of a woman's clothing on hangers, some hat boxes on a shelf.

Odd, he thought. The armoire, which had appeared to be a free-standing piece, was not. It was attached to the wall behind it. McLean tapped the back panel lightly. Listened to the hollow sound. Stared at the panel stupidly.

Several minutes later he pressed a raised block set into the wall—it had been concealed by the hat boxes on the high shelf—and the panel creaked open.

McLean stepped through the wall into a narrow, dusty, cobwebbed passage. Reaching back, he pushed the hat boxes back in place, concealing the inset block that opened the secret door. Then he closed the armoire's outer doors and the back panel, sealing himself in the tiny passageway in total darkness, so black that after a few moments he began to feel disoriented and nearly lost his balance.

The secret passage must lead somewhere, he thought, but he could not find another opening or exit. Or was it a blind hidey-hole, built into the house over a hundred years ago?

He heard a key turn in a lock, the rasp of metal on metal startlingly loud and clear. Then frantic footsteps, doors banging. "My God! He's gone!"

"He can't be!"

"He is! See for yourself—the bastard's gone!"

"He's got to be here somewhere. Look, the windows are all locked on the inside. The doors were both locked. There's no way he could have got out."

Silence then. McLean waited, heart thumping so loudly that he was sure they would hear it if they just stopped to listen.

The doors of the armoire opened. Only the thin back panel stood between McLean and the two boys with the baseball bats.

"He's not in there, there's no room." McLean immediately attached the deep, rumbling voice to the hairy-chested giant.

"Oh shit! Stacy's going to kill me!"

"We shouldn't have got into this stuff, Brad."

"She's my sister! What was I gonna do? Besides, you heard what kind of creep this guy is."

"He didn't act like any hit man for the Mob."

"How are they supposed to act, man? Shit, Freddy, he's not going to come up to you and show you his gun."

"He didn't have a gun," Freddy the giant pointed out.

The doors to the armoire closed, making their voices a little less distinct. The voices kept fading away and coming back like weak signals from an underpowered radio station. Stacy Barrett's brother said, "He must be some kind of Houdini. There's no way he could've got out of here."

"Maybe he picked the lock, got into the bathroom, locked the door again behind him. It doesn't use a key."

Brad considered this. When he spoke again there was a new nervousness in his voice. "He might still be in the house."

"Yeah." Freddy didn't sound as worried. "We'll have to search it."

"Oh shit, it's a big house! Maybe we should just get the hell out of here."

"She's your sister," Freddy said. "You want to tell her we let him get away?" There was a long pause before the deep voice rumbled on. "You never said, what was she gonna do with him, anyway? I figured we'd just beat the shit out of him and stuff him in a trash can somewheres, teach the son of a bitch a lesson. Why did Stacy want to keep him here?"

"I don't know." There was a trace of a whine in Brad's tone, making McLean think of Bill Cosby's brain-damaged-kids routine. *I don't know . . .*

There was a silence so prolonged that McLean began to wonder if the two youths had left the room. Then Freddy said, very clearly, "We better start looking for him before *he* finds *us.*"

"You realize how many *rooms* there are in this goddamn mausoleum?"

"We better start at the top and work down. Stick together and keep your eyes open."

"He was hurt," Brad said. "I don't think he'd hang around. He's gone, man."

"We were downstairs all the time," Freddy rumbled.

"He's a Houdini," Stacy Barrett's brother complained.

Their voices faded away once more, and there was silence. In the pitch-black secret passageway, McLean brushed cobwebs from his face and leaned against a wall. He hadn't wanted to move a muscle while the two bat swingers were on the other side of the thin panel. A cramp had started in his left calf, and now he kneaded it with his good right hand, letting the fingers bite deep into the tight muscle.

Brad wanted to leave, McLean thought. How long would Freddy be able to keep him there searching?

McLean settled down to wait. He began a slow, careful flexing of his muscles, trying to work out some of the stiffness and soreness. He lost all sense of time in the isolating darkness. Even the storm was inaudible except for some distant muttering of thunder. Sometimes he heard footsteps—at first on the floor overhead, then not far away on the second story. The old house creaked and groaned and whispered.

McLean thought of being trapped in this hidey-hole like a victim in a horror novel, not being able to fight his way out, remaining sealed in forever. He had to choke back a wave of claustrophobia, panic making his heart thud wildly.

The two young men never came back.

An hour later, perhaps two—there was no measure of time in that smothering darkness—McLean tested the secret panel at the back of the armoire. It opened easily.

The storm still raged outside. Rain lashed at the windows, distant thunder rumbled, lightning revealed the outlines of the shaded windows in brief flashes like a laser light show.

McLean tried one of the windows. It was frozen shut by layers of old paint. He didn't fancy the drop from a second-story window in his present condition, anyway.

His eyes adjusted to darkness, he was able to see surprisingly well. He stepped into the hall and stood motionless. Light filtered along the corridor from a deep window at the front of the house that flooded the staircase with light during the day, and from another window, tall and narrow, at the back of the hall.

He found the back stairway. It made a single turn and led down to the back of the house.

He went down a step at a time, testing each one before letting his weight descend on it, fearing the squeaks and groans of the old house. One step emitted an audible creak, causing him to freeze. He remained still for a full minute. Nothing happened.

The rest of the way down was noiseless. A doorway at the bottom of the stairs opened into a small back hall next to the kitchen. An outside door faced the back yard.

Had they given up the search and left?

McLean crept back through the house. All the rooms were dark. No one was there. He wondered if anyone lived in the house, or if it was now, after a hundred years or more, only for display, awaiting the conversion to apartments. The other grand houses selected for the tour had all been currently occupied, open only for the tour.

Stacy Barrett had known this one was unoccupied.

He was in the great hall at the front of the house, near the foot of the main staircase, when the telephone shrilled.

McLean jumped a foot. Hair rose at the back of his neck. He fell back against the wall, heart racing.

The telephone nearest him was on a long, narrow table set against the wall in the front hall under the stairs. McLean stared at it, counting the rings. Six, seven . . . nine . . . eleven . . . The caller gave up at last. Fifteen rings.

Someone was supposed to be here to answer.

McLean tiptoed back through the house, making no noise although he now believed the house to be empty. The back door had a security throwbolt that opened by means of a thumb latch, not a key. One of the multiple Victorian porches of the house wrapped around the back and offered cover from the rain when McLean stepped out through the door.

Outside the house, the storm came alive in all its awesome fury. Lightning danced and flickered, bright enough to reveal the tall trees at the back of the garden, a long rose bed, a garage or storage building at the back of the lot. Thunder crashed, loud enough to shake the earth.

McLean waited for another lightning flash to reveal a brick path leading toward the rear of the garden. He jumped off the porch and dashed along the path. He was instantly drenched.

A floodlight came on at the back of the house. Running figures splashed toward him into the light. They carried baseball bats in their hands.

McLean slipped on the wet bricks, caught his balance after sloshing through a puddle, and ran on. The nearer of the two figures racing after him, each of whom had been concealed under the roof of the wide porch at a corner of the house, was the smaller of the boys, Stacy's brother Brad. He was running across the lawn at an angle that would bring him close to McLean at the end of the rose bed.

McLean calculated his chances, taking his battered condition into account. At the end of the rose bed he made a sudden sharp turn, veering directly toward Brad.

The move caught the youth by surprise. He was quick enough to swing his bat in a vicious, chopping stroke, but McLean came in low, under the swinging bat. He drove his shoulder into Brad's stomach and lifted. Breath exploded from the young man's lungs. McLean completed the lift and throw in one motion, tossing Brad on his back into the rose bed. Brad cried out as thorns raked his flesh.

Then McLean was running again, dodging away from Freddy the giant, who slipped when he tried to make a quick cut to intercept him. A five-foot board fence framed the lot, and McLean vaulted it in one spring, hands atop the fence. He barely cleared it, his back leg scraping. Freddy had more trouble hoisting his considerable weight over the fence. By the time he had a leg over the top McLean was through a gate at the end of the adjoining property and racing along the back street.

The rain lashed at him, slowing him down. He turned left at the first street, heading away from the river. Two houses along the way, he ran in between the buildings, trotted through another long yard, climbed another fence, and threaded through a formal garden. He emerged from the shadows of a house onto the next street.

He had been in comparatively good shape before the beating. Now his legs and arms were leaden, and he stumbled as he ran.

At a corner, under the protection of a great old pine that kept off some of the downpour, he stopped to look back. The storm soaked up most of the light from the gas lamps, and he could see little. He stayed motionless, his shadow merging with that of the tree, for several minutes.

Brad and Freddy never appeared. McLean listened to the rain and the thunder and laughed aloud. It was the damned storm, he thought. They had hidden on the porch, waiting for him to show himself, keeping dry. They hadn't wanted to get wet, and they had quickly abandoned the chase.

He turned along the tree-shaded street, still moving away from the river, his thoughts now reviewing the sketch map of Riverton he had kept in his mind, considering how to find his own shelter from the storm.

He wondered who had been telephoning the house just before he left.

12

THERE WERE THREE of the old-fashioned gas street lights to a long block. Their flickering glow through the thinning rain was undoubtedly picturesque, though McLean was not in a mood to appreciate the atmospheric effect. *Gaslight*, he thought. The name of the old movie popped into his mind. Showing his age, he thought.

What little thunder and lightning remained of the storm had moved off to the east, which lit up now and then like a backdrop. The sky, still heavy with clouds, had lifted somewhat and was less ominously black. The rain fell in a gentle patter among the trees.

The road McLean followed brought him to Main Street. Under the last of the gas lights he checked his watch: 10:40. He had lost about eleven hours since Stacy Barrett invited him into the back bedroom.

Along Main Street he took shelter briefly in the entry of a

small craft and hobby shop and another store next to it. When he moved further along the street and stopped in the covered entry of a third store, he saw a small sign in the window: *Second Best. Items Old and New.*

He peered inside. The store was dark, but enough light filtered in from the street to reveal clusters of furniture, small appliances and glassware and other household items on long tables, a litter of knickknacks on other tables, clothing hanging on pipe-iron racks.

Shivering in his wet clothes, McLean found that the simple lock on the door had no deadbolt. The lock yielded easily to a plastic credit card. He opened the door and stepped inside.

The store smelled musty. His wet shoes squished in the silence as he made his way along the aisles. At the back of the store he found a rack of men's slacks, another of shirts and jackets. After emptying his pockets and placing their contents on the corner of a long table, he quickly stripped off his soaking garments. He found a pair of Jockey shorts in an unopened package, a set of three brand-new white tube socks in another plastic wrapper. The shorts were a size small but blessedly dry. He gratefully slipped one pair of the thick athletic socks on his feet and temporarily stuffed another pair of socks into his shoes to soak up some of the moisture. Then he tried on four pairs of size thirty-six slacks from one of the racks until he found one that was a passable fit. They were a tan corduroy, softened with wear. He transferred his wallet and change—his money and identification were untouched—to the Second Best slacks. He reflected that he might have avoided a lot of trouble if he had kept his Redfern identification in his wallet instead of the substitute driver's license and credit cards bearing David Patterson's name. Or would Stacy Barrett have believed that Redfern's identification cards had been stolen from a murdered man?

Over the slacks McLean donned a clean, long-sleeved shirt

and a bulky sweater. After a few minutes in the dry clothes and warm sweater he stopped shivering.

Off in a corner of the store he found a cracked leather sofa and stretched out on it. The rain had died to a whisper now. He could hear an occasional car swish by along Broad Street. Otherwise the night was quiet and peaceful. His head hammered and, now that he had stopped moving around, all of his assorted aches and sores made themselves felt.

He sat up. Another car drove along the wet street, its headlights sweeping past the secondhand goods store. It was on Main Street, moving at a crawl.

McLean watched from the shadows of the store. The car cruised slowly up to Broad Street, stopped there for what seemed a long time. Then it backed up and made a U-turn. It returned along Main. When it drifted past the thrift shop McLean saw two men inside. The one on the near side, in the passenger's seat, filled the car's side window with his bulk.

The car drove on down the street, its red taillights eventually dimming and vanishing into the night.

McLean went back to his sofa and lay down again. It took a while for his heartbeat to slow down to normal. He tried to think about how he would find Angie now if Stacy Barrett refused to believe him. Before he could pursue the question, he fell asleep.

When he woke it was light outside. Morning. He felt a moment's alarm. How long had he slept?

His watch said 6:15. He fell back on the leather sofa, resting his head on the arm. He regretted the sudden movement when he awakened and sat up. His head pounded. The pain from his ribs was moderate except when he moved quickly or twisted his body. As for the rest—the stiffness and soreness from head to toe—that was something he would have to live with for a while.

When would the store open? Probably not for hours, although he didn't intend to stay that long.

McLean's own clothes were still wet. There was nothing about them to identify him. The once-handsome Brooks Brothers jacket was shapeless, but he supposed that it could be restored to something like its former glory if it were dry-cleaned and pressed. He decided to leave it along with his other garments in exchange for those he was now wearing. A fair bargain, he thought.

Leaving the store, he walked east in the cool of early morning along Main Street, away from the river, at a steady pace. There was some cloud cover but the storm had moved eastward. Here and there were patches of blue sky as the morning brightened. He limped at first, every bone aching, but after ten minutes or so the moderate exercise of walking worked some of the stiffness out of his bruised muscles.

About two miles from Riverton he came to another town center. He had breakfast at a small café in Cinnaminson. He lingered over the hot coffee, letting his mind and body sort out their needs at their own pace. At the cash register on his way out he asked about bus schedules. There was a bus leaving just after nine o'clock for Camden. He could catch it if he hurried.

The bus carried him into downtown Camden, where he caught another bus over the bridge to Philadelphia. It dropped him off at the Greyhound Bus Terminal only a few blocks from his hotel.

He walked along slowly, musing about the gratitude one could feel for the simple pleasures of being alive and free to go your own way. People moved briskly past him on their way to work. Many of the young women, he noticed, wore walking or jogging shoes while carrying their office dress shoes in their bags. At a busy intersection a small crowd milled around cautiously, many of them crouching or stooping to peer at the cracked sidewalk or the gutter. Some of the passersby detoured around the crowd, but as many stopped out of curiosity. "What is it? Lose something?" Someone said, as if it were the complete explanation, "Contacts." Another onlooker said, "Oh, of course!" and joined in the painstaking and fruitless search.

McLean stepped carefully around the scene, smiling in spite of himself.

He strode quickly and purposefully through the lobby of the Warwick. When an elevator opened its doors immediately before him, he breathed a sigh of relief. A gray-haired bellhop gave him a curious glance as he stepped into the elevator with some luggage. McLean got off at the fourth floor, found the stairway, and ascended one more flight to the fifth floor, where he let himself into his room at the end of the long corridor.

The room had been made up while he was gone the previous day. It appeared undisturbed since. A red light blinking on his telephone informed him that he had received a message or messages while he was out. McLean hesitated. Stacy Barrett and Ralph Hamilton of the *Inquirer* were supposedly the only ones who knew he was staying at the Warwick. He wasn't ready for either.

Ignoring the winking red light, he ran hot water into the tub while he stripped off his borrowed clothes and made a bundle of them, separating the thick white socks and the bulky sweater. When the tub was full enough he eased his bruised body into the hot water and stretched out as much as he could. For twenty minutes, until the water began to cool, he soaked away the aches and stiffness. Then he climbed out, dried himself, and fell naked into the inviting bed.

He woke at one o'clock, shaved, dressed in his own clothes, and picked up the phone to retrieve his messages.

*   *   *

"Where the hell have you been, Barney?" In his agitation Paul Thornton sounded angry.

"Busy."

"We were waiting for you to call all day yesterday. Zeller put a man on the phone here all night, and I didn't sleep much. You wouldn't give us any way to get hold of you, and then when you didn't call . . . Christ, Barney—"

"How's Janie, Paul?"

"What?" The question brought Thornton up short. After a brief silence he said sheepishly, "She's fine. Worried about Linda being over in Europe this summer. She's afraid Linda will be kidnapped by terrorists, or worse. You know how mothers are."

"Yes, I know." McLean thought of Angie's fight to hold on to her son. "Is Zeller there?"

"No, he's not. He was called away on another assignment. There's more going on here than your little adventure, Barney."

McLean reflected briefly on his situation as a "little adventure." He asked, "What was so urgent that it couldn't wait, Paul?"

"It's what you asked Zeller for! I hope you know what the hell you're doing, Barney. This business about Marchetti gets kind of sticky."

"Zeller was able to get to him?"

"That's not the problem. Hell, he's in the phone book, he's a businessman."

"Then what's the problem?"

"Those people expect quid pro quo, Barney, you know that. They do you a favor, they want you to know it in case they might come back to you."

"I'm not asking Marchetti for any favors, I just want to talk to him."

"That's the favor," Thornton said. "And it isn't you he expects to pay it back, it's us."

"I'll get to him in my own way, then," McLean said tersely, irritated.

"No, no, it's all set up!" Thornton said quickly. "That's why we were so anxious to get hold of you. It's set for tomorrow night—Friday night. The old man always eats out on Friday night, different places. He doesn't say where, but we've got it set so a car will pick you up at your hotel and—"

"How'd you know I was staying at a hotel, Paul?"

"I know *you*, Barney. You never liked motels."

McLean was silent for a moment. Thornton had been ready with his answer. Perhaps too quick.

"Just let us know where to have the car come and we'll tell Marchetti."

"No, give me a number where I can reach him or leave a message. I'll tell him where I'll be at the last minute. Or meet him wherever he says."

"This is ridiculous, Barney!" Thornton protested. "You can trust our arrangements."

"No," said McLean. "*That* would be ridiculous."

There was a long silence at the other end of the line. McLean gave his old friend time to sort out his ruffled feathers. They knew where he was, he thought. They had had plenty of time to set up a trace on his calls.

"Okay, if that's the way you want it."

"That's the way I want it, Paul. Nothing personal."

"Yeah. Just a minute, I'll get you a number . . ." Thornton came back on the line after a short delay and read off a phone number, prefixing it with the Philadelphia area code. He repeated the number and asked, "You got that?"

"I've got it, thanks. Tell Zeller I'll be in touch again . . . after I've seen Tony Marchetti."

"You shouldn't be doing this on your own." Thornton's tone had thawed a little, but he wasn't quite over his pique.

"The Agency threw me out on my own," McLean said sharply. "And you've left me there while one of your favorite gunfighters has gone ape."

"Nobody's given Coffey the green light!" Paul Thornton protested. "He . . . he's out of control."

"Then get a straightjacket for him. Or I will."

He had hardly hung up when the phone rang. He gave it a half-dozen rings before picking up the receiver. His mind was still chasing after any hidden nuances in the conversation with Thornton.

"Mr. McLean? Are you there?" The voice belonged to Stacy Barrett.

"Good as new."

"Oh thank God! I was afraid . . . I didn't know where you were, what had happened to you."

"I appreciate your concern, Mrs. Barrett."

The pause was awkward, prickly with unvoiced angers and regrets. "I deserve that, I know." Stacy sounded positively demure. "But you have to understand my position. How was I to know you were who you said you were? I told you, Louis Marchetti has tried such ruses before."

"I understand," said McLean patiently.

"I . . . I hope you do. Are you all right? I tried to call the house last night after I saw Angie. I wanted to . . . to stop things. I was too late, you'd already escaped. I was terrified, not knowing what had happened. I hope those boys didn't . . . I mean . . ."

"They did the best they could." McLean let her suffer a little. She seemed to be good at it. "There are no bones broken, Mrs. Barrett, maybe a couple of cracks, that's all. At least nothing that won't heal. And I don't plan on seeing a lawyer."

She covered her nervousness with a brittle little laugh. "I'm happy you can joke about it."

"So am I."

"Angie was beside herself after I showed her the Polaroid snapshot and told her what I'd done. She was frightened and . . . very angry."

"She probably thought you should have shown her the picture before sending in the batters," McLean suggested.

"I . . . I really don't know what to say. Except that . . . I'm terribly sorry."

McLean wondered how much that apology had cost her. Stacy Barrett had rarely, he was sure, been called upon to use those words.

"The boys pulled their punches a little," he said after a time. "They didn't have their hearts in it."

"They're good kids," Stacy said earnestly. "They really are. They were doing it because I asked them. I told them just enough so they would understand it was . . . important."

McLean smiled at her earnestness. "I guess Brad admires his big sister too much to turn her down."

"Yes . . . well . . ." She didn't like him knowing that one of his attackers had been her brother. "I'd like to make it up to you, Mr. McLean."

"There is one way."

"I know. Can you meet me Saturday for lunch?"

The abrupt question caught McLean by surprise. "Why Saturday? Why so long?"

"Angie isn't in town. It will take me a little time to arrange things. We still have to be careful, Mr. McLean. Not of you," she added hastily.

McLean didn't like it but there seemed to be little he could say that would change the decision. "All right, where shall I meet you?"

"At Wanamaker's," she said. "Downtown. In the Crystal Room at twelve o'clock. Do you know it?"

"I'll find it," said McLean. "Will Angie be with you?"

There was the briefest hesitation before Stacy Barrett said, "She'll be there. She's just as anxious as you are, Mr. McLean."

"Then tell her to take a tranquilizer."

Stacy Barrett rewarded him with a generous laugh. "I'll tell her. Oh, there is one other thing you should know . . . Someone else called, asking me about you. A man." She gave another warm chuckle. "I suppose it must be a friend. He knows all about those different names you use."

McLean felt a chill at the back of his neck. "I don't suppose *he* gave a name."

"As a matter of fact, he didn't. But I didn't tell him anything about you," she added quickly.

"Can you tell me exactly what you said?"

"Well . . . that I had heard from you but didn't know you at all and wouldn't have anything to do with you."

"Mmm." McLean considered the possibilities. There weren't many. "Thank you, Mrs. Barrett. If he calls again, or anyone else calls, say the same thing."

"Yes, of course. Is anything wrong . . . anything we should know about?"

"Saturday," said McLean. "Tell Angie, after Saturday . . . no more secrets."

It was a promise he meant to keep.

13

THE CONFRONTATION WITH Clark Coffey was drawing nearer. Soon, now. Perhaps it had always been destined, and in running away from it he had only been postponing the inevitable.

McLean glanced around his hotel room. *I know you, Barney, you never liked motels.* He cursed his own stupidity. He knew better. He knew that most people, even someone on the run, tended to repeat themselves, to follow familiar paths of behavior. A ruse that had worked once would work again. A favorite hideout or place to spend the night would be chosen again. An experienced stalker relied on patterns. McLean was known to have a liking for smaller, older hotels with touches of almost forgotten luxury, as opposed to the sleek, homogenized efficiency of most modern motels.

That fact would be in his file.

Coffey—or someone friendly to him—could have had access to everything in that file.

McLean began a methodical examination of his room, as opposed to the cursory inspection he had given it on his return. Before leaving he had given no thought to the elementary trade-craft of placing invisible clues to intrusion—a hair over the top of the door or across a corner of his suitcase that would be displaced should either be disturbed. Such procedures were useless in a hotel room where a cleaning maid routinely entered each day.

However, in spite of being out of touch for the past three years, McLean still did some things automatically. He had aligned his shaving kit, for example, with a crack in the wall above it. The kit was on a glass shelf where the maid had no reason to disturb it. He had also aligned the suitcase on its portable rack so that its edge was exactly parallel with the side of the dresser. Both the shaving kit and the suitcase had been moved slightly out of position. The maid? Or someone else?

Going to the window, McLean stood slightly to the side and gazed down at Seventeenth Street, taking in the shops and offices across the way, the small café, the street vendors and pedestrians. He gave particular attention to one building to his left, just beyond a narrow alleyway. Like most such alleys in downtown Philadelphia, it was a functioning street with a few doorways opening off it.

McLean bundled a few clothes and toiletries together, placed them in a plastic cleaning bag he found in the dresser drawer, made a quick visual survey of the room once more, and left. He did not take his suitcase or most of his clothes with him. In addition to slowing him down, the suitcase would make him too conspicuous. Besides, leaving most of his clothing and his suitcase in the room would reinforce the impression that he had not left the hotel. Nor would he check out.

Ignoring the elevator, he walked down the five flights of stairs to the main floor, exiting out of view of the lobby. Not that there was room for Coffey to hang around inconspicuously in the small lobby, but he might linger in the coffee shop or at the bar where he could see anyone coming or going. McLean left the hotel through the back hallway to the garage. There he stood behind a row of cars against the back wall, analyzing the possibilities.

From what Stacy Barrett had said, by now Coffey almost certainly knew the name he was using. That meant he could have learned where McLean was staying simply by calling certain types of hotels. He would have verified the fact that McLean had kept a car in the Warwick's garage. He would know that the car was not there now, so there was no reason for him to wait inside the garage, even if he could manage to get in without being seen. From the garage he could not monitor the lobby entrance. He would want to be in a position to see McLean entering the hotel or his car returning to the garage. He had to be out front.

A coffee shop across the way. A store or an office in the same block with a window facing the street. A rooftop, but that seemed unlikely, since there was nothing suitable across the way that would not make a watcher attract the attention of those on the hotel's upper floors.

McLean strode through the garage, nodding at one of the attendants on his way out, and emerged into the alley. To the right was Seventeenth Street and the front of the hotel. If Coffey had a stakeout in place, he would see McLean emerge from the alley.

McLean turned left. There were a few shops along the alley but none looked promising. The alley led him through to Eighteenth Street opposite Rittenhouse Square, with its chic boutiques and offices and galleries, its joggers and strollers and lovers. McLean crossed the street and trotted along a diagonal path through the tree-shaded park. Looking back on the far side, he saw no one following him.

Following Nineteenth Street over to Sansom, McLean turned east along the narrow street. He paused for a few minutes in a book store, watching the sidewalk out front while he appeared to browse through some books at a remainder table. Then he continued along the street and stepped into the Commissary.

He ate downstairs—a delicious rice and barley soup, a roll and coffee—at one of the small tables. The self-service restaurant was small, crowded, and friendly. It reminded McLean of places he had favored years ago.

Reassured that Coffey had not spotted him leaving the Warwick, McLean caught a bus on Chestnut Street over to Old Town and the river. He walked past Penn's Landing to the parking lot where, embarking on the Open House tour the previous morning, he had left his rented Chevrolet.

This time he checked into the Quality Inn on Twenty-second Street and was given a room overlooking the Benjamin Franklin Parkway, a broad boulevard bordered by parks with cascades of trees and flowers in bloom that reminded McLean a little of the Champs-Elysees. The Rodin Museum was across the way from his hotel, the grand old Philadelphia Museum of Art was within easy walking distance to the west.

He rested, soaked his bruises in another hot bath, and had dinner that evening at a restaurant within the hotel. Afterward he lay on his bed, waiting for darkness. He thought of Clark Coffey stalking him across the country. Of the obsession that drove him in his pursuit.

Conflict within the Agency was hardly new; it was almost endemic. Given the egos involved and the unnatural pressures of much of the work, it could hardly be otherwise. That conflict was seldom, however, lethal.

McLean had fought in Laos and Vietnam with the Agency. He had not been involved with the Phoenix Project, which had won so much notoriety in later years. Then or later, McLean had felt no sympathy for the Ban-an-minh, whose capacity for torture and cruelty and murder was boundless, who in a sense had laid the ground rules for their own secret conflict with the agents of Phoenix. At the same time, McLean was disgusted by those on his own side who lost control, who destroyed or killed indiscriminately. When men in battle set aside all the rules so painfully constructed over centuries of civilization, there was no defense. No honor.

During his years within the Agency McLean had watched it change while its internal struggles went on. Part of the change was the drift toward technical surveillance and information-gathering as opposed to dependence on human resources—on spies and informants and double-agents. But part of it was the hardening conflict between opposing views within the Agency, between the moderates and the Cold Warriors, between those who saw their role as carrying out policies of elected officials and those who had become so obsessed with their mission that they had determined to become a power unto themselves. These were the agents who inspired or carried out coups without directives from the President. Who plotted bizarre assassinations. Who acted against U.S. citizens within their own country. An excess of self-righteousness combined with power, McLean thought, was as dangerous as any drug.

Carl Warner had been one of the zealots. He had an army of friends within the Agency, those who had grown tired of losing, or who had come to despise the cruelty and duplicity of the "evil empire" they saw as the ultimate enemy. There were just as many who opposed the Cold Warriors, but their opposition came in the form of questions, doubts, objections, civilized debate. The zealots always brought more passion to their arguments and actions.

Clark Coffey was not only the best of Carl Warner's protégés, trained and indoctrinated by him. He was also a killing machine, a sociopath who should never have been provided the cloak of sanction that came with employment by the Agency in the field.

Eric Zeller was no fanatic. He was an ambitious man, McLean believed, but a realist. He saw his authority as coming down through the DCI from the President. The Agency served the administration and the country in the best way it could. Zeller saw that service as important, even essential, and he would therefore do anything to keep the Agency from being damaged. Zeller did not condone or sanction Clark Coffey's murderous quest for vengeance, but his reaction was more one of administrative dismay and personal distaste than moral outrage.

McLean was convinced that Zeller would try to stop Coffey. He was equally certain that Zeller would fail.

But if that were true . . . who was helping Coffey?

When it was dark McLean left his room and went down to the hotel garage. There he located the attendant he had talked to on his arrival, a young man who would be going off duty at nine o'clock. McLean repeated his earlier instructions, reminded the young man, who had a thick shock of red hair, that he should not wear a cap or hat, and that he should make himself immediately conspicuous once he arrived at the Warwick's garage. "You got it, man!" the redhead said cheerfully. A twenty-dollar tip for driving a car a distance of no more than twenty-five blocks added to his good cheer.

McLean had convinced himself that there was no risk to the young man. Coffey was not going to try random sniping in the middle of downtown Philadelphia without identifying the driver of the car. The attack in Newport Beach, risking the lives of innocent bystanders, had been impetuous. Coffey had had time to plan his next attack. He would not make the same mistake twice. He would not miss again.

Before he left the Warwick McLean had picked out his own vantage point. It was an office building across the way, just past the alley, with shops on the street level, offices and a few other stores above.

McLean approached the building from the east, past St. Mark's Church. The only risk, he thought as he let himself into the building by means of a service door off the alley, would come if Coffey had by chance chosen the same lookout.

The shop McLean had chosen was on the second floor. It was dark, closed for the night, but he had no trouble picking the lock. He had visited the shop once in the past, intrigued by the selection of old and out-of-print books. A littered desk was placed almost in the wide front window, with a high-backed chair behind it facing away from the light. The stacks of old books on all sides and piled in heaps on the floor deepened the gloom, allowing little penetration of light from the street or the hotel across the way.

McLean settled down in the darkness to wait.

At 9:15 the Chevrolet Celebrity nosed into the alley next to the Warwick Hotel from Seventeenth Street and drove at a sedate pace along the alley to the garage entrance. McLean stood next to the window of the bookshop, eyes scanning the street. At first there was nothing unusual, no sudden or hurried movement. Then a man appeared on the sidewalk almost directly below McLean's lookout point. The figure dodged through traffic across Seventeenth and hurried along the alley. A tall man. Broad-shouldered. Quick, sure-footed movements. He disappeared along the alley, keeping close to the wall, and was soon lost in shadows.

McLean let out a breath of relief a few moments later when the redheaded garage attendant from the Quality Inn emerged from the Warwick's lobby, exchanged a grin and a few words with the doorman on the sidewalk, and stood waiting by the curb until another car swerved toward him and pulled up, a convertible sports car driven by a young woman. The redhead jumped in without bothering to open the car door, and the little car shot off from the curb at the same moment Clark Coffey reappeared at the head of the alley.

Coffey stared along the street after the sports car. Then he looked up at the windows of the hotel. At a window on the fifth floor, McLean thought.

He waited a half-hour before he left the way he had come. He walked down to Broad Street, where he caught a taxi in front of the Academy of Music.

Back in his room at the Quality Inn he gazed thoughtfully down at the traffic along the wide boulevard. Soon, he thought. He and Coffey in a head-on collision, one on one. It had to come.

But first he must see Angie safe. Angie and young Tony.

Making that possible had to begin not with Louis Marchetti but with the father. With Old Tony Marchetti. He took the slip of paper from his pocket on which he had written the phone number Paul Thornton gave him.

14

Old TONY MARCHETTI HAD A VOICE like gravel pouring down a metal chute. "Why should I talk to you?" he asked.

"I believe some mutual friends have already been in touch with you."

"We got no mutual friends."

"From Washington," said McLean.

Old Tony wheezed into the phone for a moment. Then he grunted and said, "Those aren't friends."

"They might be useful sometime."

"With people like that I got no use. You are wasting your time, McLean. And mine."

"I've been living with your daughter-in-law, Mr. Marchetti."

There was a long pause. Marchetti hadn't known, McLean thought. Finally the old man said, "You want to see me to tell me that? That my Angie been living in sin with you? You got a death wish, McLean."

"I didn't force her to stay with me. She was there out of love."

"Love, is it? I will show you love, McLean. That girl is like my own flesh and blood. Don't you talk to me about living in sin with her!"

McLean frowned. He stared out of his hotel window at the morning traffic. He had made one call the night before, trying to reach Marchetti, but he had been told bluntly that Old Tony was not available that night—not to anyone, not even the Pope himself. Listening to the old man's harsh voice now, he heard unexpected anguish. It might prove to be a barrier—or a way to reach him.

"I will tell you how your daughter is," McLean said quietly. "And your grandson Tony, how he is. How things were with us, and what we hope for the future. But we may need your help, Mr. Marchetti. Angie does, and Tony, if they are to have any future at all."

"What is it you're saying?" Marchetti said ominously.

"I think you know. Angie has been in hiding with Tony. Your son Louis found where we were living together. He sent two men to bring them back. One was from the East and one from Las Vegas. These men were . . . I think you would call them soldiers. Heavy hitters."

"I know nothing of this!"

"They came for her, and she ran."

"And you," Old Tony said skeptically. "You met these men? You talked to them? You know what names they have?"

"I met them, but we didn't talk much. One of them was called Raymond Ryder. The other was Benny Popolano."

Old Tony was silent. "I knew Benny," he said. "I did not know this other one. Where are these men now, these . . . heavy hitters?"

"They're dead."

There was another long silence. McLean could hear Old Tony

wheezing into the phone. He sounded as if he had asthma or emphysema. Stress made either condition worse, McLean thought. "You are a serious man, McLean," the old man said at length.

"It is a serious matter."

"I will talk with you. This was arranged for tonight by those people from Washington, but I had to be sure. Where are you? I will send a car."

"At the Quality Inn Center City," said McLean.

"This is not what I was told," Old Tony said.

"I've moved." McLean was hardly surprised by the confirmation that mutual friends in Washington had been able to tell Marchetti he was at the Warwick. "I'm now at the Quality Inn."

"Seven o'clock, McLean. A black car. You will be waiting?"

"I'll be ready, Mr. Marchetti. I'll find it."

"They will find you," Old Tony said.

The big black car was a stretch Lincoln Continental limousine. The chauffeur wore a dark gray uniform with a black tie and a visored cap. The bulky man who climbed out of the cavernous interior and sought out McLean with hooded eyes wore a rumpled seersucker suit with a red striped tie. McLean, who had neither a suit nor a tie, wondered if he was properly dressed for the occasion in his Second Best thrift shop bulky sweater over slacks and loafers. Perhaps he should have kept his Brooks Brothers jacket.

When they were in the car and moving, the bulky man turned in the seat to face McLean. He did it as if he had a stiff neck, swiveling his upper body without turning his head. "You understand, I have to be sure you're not carrying."

McLean nodded his understanding. He had known better than

to bring his Colt Magnum along to a meeting with a Mafia don. He submitted to a quick, hands-on body search. Sleepy Eyes was anything but sleepy in his thoroughness. "Good," he said when he had finished. "Mr. Marchetti said you were a serious man."

McLean said nothing.

The restaurant, which was in South Philly not far from the Italian Market, was old, Italian, unpretentious on the outside, in poor taste on the inside where fake stone, too much wrought iron, and red vinyl booths reached for grandeur and failed. The place had also grown haphazardly, leading to a chopped-up, add-on effect. It was also warm, friendly and engagingly gregarious. A family place, McLean thought. Probably started small, serving neighborhood Italians, and simply grew with the city, its reputation spreading. Still a family restaurant, or so it appeared. The young host with all the flashing white teeth would be an older son, daughter was at the cash register, mama still overseeing the kitchen, papa moving among his friends and customers to exchange greetings.

Old Tony Marchetti was in a separate area at the back that served as a bar. It had a lot of dark wood, a long bar with a brass rail and an elaborate mirrored back-bar, and more of the red vinyl booths. The room was not really separate, being set off only by a partition with some turned wooden posts. Old Tony was given the privacy that was his due without being cut off from the sights and sounds of the restaurant.

The young host with the teeth was expecting McLean and his bodyguard, and he escorted them promptly to the back corner where Old Tony waited, already sampling the antipasto and some dark red wine. "Sit down, McLean," he gestured. The burly bodyguard withdrew without a word, leaving the two men alone.

The booth was spacious, and there was plenty of room for

McLean to sit directly facing the old man. It was the first time, he reflected with irony, that he had ever dined with an authentic Syndicate boss. A boss among bosses.

"I have ordered for us," Old Tony said, his black eyes shrewd, hard, coldly appraising. "The mussels you must try. Mama also makes her own pasta, and the veal scaloppine would make a saint weep. You don't mind my ordering?"

"Not at all."

Old Tony nodded. "Have some wine. Those little things, they have crab inside. Delicious. This is real food, McLean, not that French shit. You understand?"

McLean smiled, wondering why he was being given the treatment. He was not the bearer of glad tidings . . .

Though he sat behind the formica table with his belly thrust up against it, and you could not say for certain how tall he was, McLean judged Old Tony to be about five-seven and fat, but big beneath the fatty layers, with a large-boned frame. His hands were huge, meaty, almost square, with blunt fingers with the nails chewed down to the quick. Although he had to be pushing seventy, Old Tony still had a full shock of hair, all of it white. His skin was swarthy, lips full like his son's, features coarse and heavy. His ears had very long lobes. McLean wondered about the mother who had given Louis Marchetti his handsome looks. Someone who had been like Angie in her youth, slim and pretty and dark-haired? Then he wondered what Louis had inherited from his father. The amoral streak of viciousness?

Old Tony lit a filtered cigarette, revealing old nicotine stains on his fingers. "You don't mind? I can't give them up. Believe me, I have tried."

"I gave them up a while back. It's not easy."

Old Tony blew smoke at the ceiling, which he studied as if it were something Michelangelo had painted. "You are a cop?" he asked abruptly.

"No."

"You work for the government? For those friends in Washington?"

McLean shook his head.

Old Tony scowled at him. He reached for some of the antipasto, chewed, smoked, and glared. "They know you."

"I used to work for the Agency," McLean said. "That was a few years back. We had a disagreement."

"What do you do now, McLean?"

"I work for an insurance company out in California."

Interest quickened in the black eyes, visible for only an instant before he blinked away the reaction. "So Angie was living in California. It was a good place for Tony?"

"Very good."

Old Tony grunted. "And you work for the insurance? Is that what you want to sell me, McLean? Insurance?"

"I'm not selling anything. I just wanted you to know why I am here in Philadelphia."

"This should concern me?"

"It concerns your son Louis. Mostly it concerns Angie and Tony, your grandson."

"So far you have told me nothing," Old Tony said. He glanced up as the waiter hovered nearby. The old man nodded and the waiter began clearing away the antipasto to make room for the main dishes, huge platters of mussels and pasta and veal in a sauce and great chunks of Italian bread. "Now we will eat," Old Tony said. "I don't talk business while I am eating. It interferes with the digestion."

They ate in silence. Somewhere in the background a piano started to play. The pianist had a heavy touch. At first McLean ate a little only to show respect. After sampling the delicious fare he helped himself to generous portions. No wonder Old Tony had grown layers of fat over that broad frame, he thought.

A half-hour later Old Tony Marchetti leaned back in the booth with a belch and a sigh, snapped his fingers at the waiter to clear the table, and wiped his mouth with a large white napkin. When the dishes were cleared away and coffee poured, the black eyes lifted from the table to pin McLean against the back of the booth. The eyes no longer made any pretense at amiability. Eating was a polite time. Now it was time for business. "You got five minutes to convince me I should listen to you, McLean."

"I want you to tell Louis to leave Angie and Tony alone."

Anger flared in the black eyes and brought a flush under the dark skin. "You have a lot of guts, McLean. I am a father! My son Louis is no angel, but he is my son. And Angie is his wife, young Tony is *his* son. Who are *you* to say he should leave them alone?"

"I'm someone who loves them both," McLean said. "Let me tell you a story. It's one that Angie told me, only at the time I didn't know she was talking about herself." He took the time to marshal his thoughts, knowing that the old man's patience might run out quickly. "She lost her parents, both of them, while she was still young. She was taken in by an aunt, her father's sister, an older woman with no children of her own." He paused again. "She had no children because she couldn't stand them around her. She never physically beat Angie because that wasn't the style in Main Line society, you just pushed them off on someone else. But the aunt approved of severe discipline for the girl. She tyrannized Angie in ways other than physical abuse, with coldness, rejection, indifference, an adult's scorn. Luckily for Angie, she spent most of her teenage years away from her aunt, in private schools. But she grew up knowing the scars that could be left on a child raised under adult tyranny, without love. She didn't want her son to grow up that way."

Old Tony's anger exploded. His big right hand banged down on the table. Dishes jumped and a water glass spilled over. A waiter rushed in to mop up the water. Old Tony ignored him. "Maybe you got guts, McLean, but you don't have the brains of a fish. You think you can tell me these things and walk away from this room without having your legs broken? You are interfering in my family! You are saying things—"

"—that you don't want to hear!" McLean cut in. "But they are things you know. *You* know!"

The old man sucked in his breath with a hissing sound. Then he wheezed alarmingly. His eyes bulged.

"Are you okay?" McLean asked anxiously.

"I am okay," Old Tony said. "You are a dead fish."

"Because I tell you the truth you already know? I don't believe that. Louis might do it, but you won't. Louis is a mean one, Mr. Marchetti. He hurts not because it is business but because he likes to hurt." He saw from the old man's eyes that the shot had struck home. Old Tony *did* know his son. "Louis beat Angie. And he slapped the boy around, terrorized him. That's one of the reasons Angie turned against him. She knew what it was like to grow up abused, and she wouldn't let it happen to her son. She had to get young Tony away from Louis."

He waited for Marchetti to react, but the old man sat silent, breathing more easily now, his eyes dangerous but unreadable. McLean took a deep breath of his own. He knew the gamble he was taking. No matter. It was a throw of the dice he had to make. "There was another reason, and I'm sure you know that one, too. Drugs."

"She turned against her own. I don't forgive that."

"She had no choice! I don't think she would have testified against him—or tried to—if it hadn't been for the way she felt about drugs. She would have tried to run away. I doubt that she would have succeeded, Louis would certainly have found her quickly if she hadn't had help. As it turned out, the government helped her, put her and the boy in the Witness Protection

Program, and it took three years before Louis found out where she was. Three years looking over her shoulder, jumping every time she saw a stranger."

"It was not right, what she did."

"You know about her brother," said McLean. "Who is to say how she should have acted? Her brother O.D.'d on cocaine. From what I'm told, she idolized the older brother, the only real family she had left, the only one who cared about her. Then she found out Louis was using their family vacations to set up drug deals."

"You don't know that." The gravel rattled more slowly down the chute of Tony Marchetti's throat. But he was listening, McLean thought. There was still a chance . . .

"Yes, I do. And so do you, Mr. Marchetti. Maybe you didn't know what Louis was up to in the beginning, but you would have found out soon enough. He started out as a banker, providing the money for big buys in South America. Then, I suppose, he saw there was a lot more to be made having his own private organization, a shadow business of his own. Bypassing your organization," McLean added.

"Go on," Old Tony said murderously. "Your time is almost up."

"He used that business-school education you staked him to, but he used it behind your back to make millions hooking kids on the playgrounds of America on drugs. He was a user himself, and"—McLean leaned forward, challenging the old man to meet his stare—"what would you bet that he didn't try to get Angie to use the stuff with him? How long would it have been, Mr. Marchetti, before he got young Tony hooked? Maybe just for laughs? How long would Tony stay clean with his own father importing, dealing, financing, and using every rotten drug that's made?"

McLean stopped. He found his heart thudding as he fought to control his own anger. Old Tony Marchetti had not interrupted, and that in itself seemed a kind of reprieve. McLean didn't know how long it would last, or what direction the next explosion might take. But there was a slackness under Old Tony's eyes and around his mouth that had not been there a moment or two ago.

Speaking more quietly, McLean said, "Angie couldn't take that risk. You're a father, you should understand why she had to do what she did. You wanted something else for your son. You didn't want him in the family business, from what I hear. You wanted him to be legitimate, a Harvard businessman, the Marchetti whose name would come to mean something besides crime and prostitution and numbers and dope. Well . . . you lost." McLean let the silence deepen. He could hear the old man's labored breathing across the table. "You lost with Louis, but you could still win. With young Tony. You can win, but there's only one way. Let Tony stay with his mother. Keep Louis away from them. Give your grandson a chance to be what you wanted his father to be."

There was a long silence. Old Tony Marchetti stared across the table at him, and the bitterness in his face was frightening. McLean found himself holding his breath. The sounds of the restaurant seemed to have faded off, isolating the two men in the back booth, but McLean knew they were being watched closely by concerned eyes, that all Old Tony had to do was lift a finger and men like the burly bodyguard would move in fast and hard. McLean shifted on the vinyl booth and winced as pain darted through his chest from the cracked rib. Another beating, he thought . . .

Old Tony said, "It is a funny thing, what a man goes after. To have a son who is . . . respected." A little of the fire flared again in the black eyes, like a small flame seen in the distance on a dark night. "I am respected, McLean. But not in . . . in that world." He shrugged the heavy shoulders. "I make no apologies. Nothing to apologize for, like that godfather in the movie. They got that part of it right. But for my son I wanted something more . . ."

"You can still have it for your grandson. He's a fine boy. Angie is a good woman, a good mother."

"And you?" the old man asked bitterly. "You would be a father to him?"

"The best I can be."

Old Tony stared at him for what seemed a long time. At last he said, "At least you are a serious man." He heaved a heavy sigh. "You know where Angie is now? And Tony?"

McLean shook his head. "They're here. I'm in contact with someone who knows where they are. I'll be seeing them. Soon, I hope."

Of a sudden the anger was gone. McLean was left sitting across from a tired old man, his face gray, jowls sagging, eyes bitter. "They're still married, you know. Louis don't give a shit about her, it's the boy he wants back. But I didn't know about the beatings. Or wanting her to put that white shit in her veins or up her nose."

"He would hit the boy sometimes, too."

"He likes being married to her because he thinks it helps him with other society broads," Old Tony said with contempt. "A married man is a safe man, Louis says. That's what he cares about being married."

McLean said nothing. Waited.

"You will find them?"

"I'll find them. What about Louis?"

"Don't ask for too much, McLean. Consider yourself a lucky man. I will not interfere if you find them and take them away. I want my grandson safe . . . even though it would mean I will not see him."

"It can be arranged. As long as no one comes hunting again."

"You ask too much. I make no promises, you understand?"

McLean studied him. The pianist on the far end of the restaurant was playing again. The crowded restaurant hubbub had returned, as if someone had just turned up the volume control. The crisis, for the moment, was over.

McLean slid out of the booth. "Thanks for dinner. When I have talked with Angie and Tony, you will hear from me."

Old Tony Marchetti watched him leave. When McLean was halfway across the restaurant the old man snapped his fingers. The burly bodyguard materialized like a magician's pawn, closing in on McLean before he reached the street.

On the sidewalk McLean turned to face him. "The car is here," the bodyguard said. "Mr. Marchetti wants I should take you back."

There could be no argument, and McLean offered none. He climbed into the stretch Lincoln and allowed himself to be driven sedately back to his hotel.

Old Tony was right, he thought as he rode. He had been very, very lucky.

15

JOHN WANAMAKER'S WAS TO DOWNTOWN Philadelphia what the old J. L. Hudson store once was to Detroit, Marshall Field's to Chicago, Bloomingdale's to New York. More than a store, it was an institution, a focal point, part of a way of life. Everything was here in one store, and with it an elegance and tradition and a sense of style impossible to find in a cloned suburban shopping mall.

On this Saturday the aisles were crowded with an Early Summer Sale in progress, clearing out all the spring fashions left over. McLean, barely glancing upward as he passed through the Grand Court, where gilded columns soared nine stories to the roof, saw crowds waiting for the elevators. Too impatient to wait, he sought out the escalators. Slower and noisier than their newer cousins, the moving stairway reminded him of the wooden escalators at the downtown J. L. Hudson store when he was a boy, when a ride on the rackety moving stairs was an adventure. He took the steps two at a time, not waiting for the escalator's leisurely pace. As he drew closer to the upper floors his heart began to hammer, not from exertion but eager anticipation.

The Crystal Room was essentially one great, open, high-ceilinged room. Paneled wooden walls set off the glitter of the huge crystal chandeliers that gave the restaurant its name. The atmosphere was gracious and quiet, of murmured conversation and softly clinking glass. Quickly scanning the sweep of tables, McLean felt sharp disappointment. Stacy Barrett was there at a table against the far wall. But she was alone.

Her smile was nervous and unexpectedly uncertain when he took a seat facing her across the table. "Where's Angie?" he asked without preamble.

"She's waiting, Mr. McLean. I . . . wanted a few minutes with you myself, if you don't mind." She smiled at his expression. "I know you're anxious. Angie's been like a schoolgirl all morning."

"But she didn't want to come up here?" He looked around the civilized room, trying to find danger. But it didn't always reveal itself, he thought.

"We decided it was too public. Someone who knew her might see her."

McLean nodded, swallowing his disappointment.

"Will you have lunch? Or a drink? I'm having a glass of wine." She indicated a crystal wine glass, half full.

"No, thanks. What did you want to talk to me about, Mrs. Barrett?"

She took a sip of wine, giving herself time to decide what she wanted to say—or rather, he thought, how to approach it.

"I've been thinking about those men in Fortune . . . the ones who tried to kill you."

"They came for Angie."

"Yes . . . they were Louis Marchetti's people, of course."

McLean said nothing, waiting for her to get to her point.

"You didn't have a gun."

"No."

Stacy Barrett nodded thoughtfully. "That's why Angie was so certain you were dead. She didn't *want* to believe it, but there seemed to be no question. And she had Tony to think of."

"I know that," said McLean. "I understand now why she ran." He paused briefly. "I'm glad to know she tried to come back."

"You had no gun, but those men were armed."

"Yes."

"And you killed them."

McLean sat back, studying her. She had got to her point, he thought.

"What kind of man are you, Mr. McLean?"

"Is it important?"

"Very."

"Does that mean you're still trying to decide for Angie?"

Stacy Barrett drew in a quick sharp breath, nostrils flaring. Men didn't talk to her that way. "I told Angie," she said after a moment's silence, "that I believe you're the kind of man she needs in her situation. A useful man to have around."

"I used to be . . ."

"A spy. Yes, Angie told me. But no longer an active one?"

"If you're wondering about the man who phoned you, asking about me, you're right, he's not a friend. And he means trouble. He's just as dangerous as Louis Marchetti, perhaps more so. But not to Angie and Tony."

She regarded him in pensive silence. Took the time to sip her white wine. Allowed her glance to stray idly toward a handsome woman sitting at a nearby table, automatically appraising the woman's dress, her hairstyle, her makeup, her jewelry, the escort with a distinguished touch of gray at his temples. Her milieu, McLean thought.

"Is that why you were in Fortune? Something like Angie's exile? Were you placed there in the Witness Protection Program?"

"Something like that."

"And . . . you're now in some danger?"

McLean smiled. "I don't seem to need old enemies for that."

"Mm." She fell silent again, started to speak, hesitated, momentarily flustered. "One of those young men in Riverton, as you know, was my brother."

"Brad? Yes, I know."

"He was there because I asked him. So was Freddy. They . . . they're not to blame for what happened. Or . . ." She shivered. "Or for what might have happened."

"Good soldiers," McLean murmured.

"What? Oh, yes . . . I see what you mean. The point is, they were doing it for me."

"And you were doing it for Angie."

"You're not angry?" She did not hide her puzzlement. He confused her.

"No," said McLean honestly. He smiled a little. "I wasn't pleased at the time."

"Yes . . . that's why I keep thinking about those two men in Fortune. Armed men . . . professionals, wouldn't you say?"

McLean shrugged. "There are no diplomas. No courses you can study."

"You killed them both," she said flatly.

"I did what I had to do."

She leaned forward, her bright, intelligent eyes searching his. "But you didn't do anything to Brad and Freddy."

"They didn't give me the chance."

"I don't think I believe that entirely. Don't forget, I was there. I think you're a professional too, Mr. McLean."

"Barney."

"Barney. You didn't really lift a hand against them, and I wanted you to know I'm grateful. Brad and Freddy are athletes. Freddy especially is very strong, but . . . they're amateurs, aren't they?"

McLean said nothing.

"I shudder to think . . ."

"Don't think about it, Mrs. Barrett."

"Stacy . . ."

"Stacy." They smiled at each other. It was more a truce, McLean thought, than genuine friendship. "It's over and done with."

"I saw the way you winced when you sat down . . . Barney. Were you badly hurt?"

"I'll be fine. No more baseball for a while though."

She laughed, relieved but still concerned. And still puzzled by the man across the table from her, a breed of man she was certain she hadn't met before.

"Where is Angie now, Stacy?"

Stacy Barrett's smile broadened into a grin. "Waiting for you downstairs."

"Where?" The eagerness made McLean's voice crack.

"On the Market Street side. I made arrangements so she could park in the delivery area." Arrangements must always have come easily for her, he thought.

"Now? She's there now?"

"Don't let me keep you . . ."

But he was already rising, hurrying across the room, not even waiting to ask where the delivery area was. He saw a row of elevators and started toward them when a pair of doors opened. Then, out of the corner of his eye, he saw the tall figure beyond the bank of elevators. Saw the arm raised as if to point at him. Saw the pistol with the exaggerated extension of the barrel that meant an attached silencer.

Clark Coffey.

He ran for the escalators, dodging as he went. The long corridor outside the Crystal Room was crowded, but the risk to innocents had not stopped Coffey firing into the crowd at John Wayne Airport.

McLean bolted past a woman at the head of the escalator, hearing her cry out, "How rude!" He went down the moving staircase three and four steps at a time. There was only one shopper on that first flight. The startled woman grabbed her handbag close as he brushed by her, thinking perhaps that he was a purse snatcher.

At the next level down McLean flashed a glance over his shoulder. Clark Coffey, pistol still raised, had just reached the top of the escalator. McLean leaped for the next escalator in the instant before Coffey's gun spat silently.

The escalator was more crowded as McLean went down. If it slowed him it would also slow Coffey, but after putting another two floors between himself and the stalking killer he decided to abandon the moving stairs. He found himself on a lower floor in a gift department. He threaded his way among the displays of china and crystal, the wall sconces and porcelain figurines and Chinese vases. Across another aisle he ducked into an area broken up into several rooms, each of which held a remarkable collection of antiques. He walked briskly but not fast enough to draw curious attention through these rooms with their softly glowing woods and gleaming brass and silver, his mind racing ahead. This floor was not as crowded as others. If it came to a shootout . . .

Far along a corridor, Coffey spotted him once more when he left the end of the antiques gallery. McLean sprinted around a corner and saw an exit sign ahead of his left. A conventional stairway.

He had had enough of escalators. He plunged down the stairs in a headlong rush, and had gained two more flights downward before he heard the door crash open above him. A bullet rang off a metal railing and whined past him to smack into the wall. Coffey's footsteps pounded down the stairs.

McLean burst out of the stairwell onto the second floor. He strode through an ornately crowned doorway into the Men's Store with its decorated ceilings, plush carpeting, a few plump chairs, understated displays of sweaters and slacks, jackets and robes . . . the London Shop, the impeccable offerings of A. Sulka & Co. . . .

On a sale table were laid out ranks of worsted and flannel slacks. As a salesman moved smilingly toward him, handlebar mustache quivering, McLean grabbed a pair of gray wool slacks, flicked a smile at the salesman, and said, "I'll just try these on."

"Oh . . . yes, sir, the fitting rooms are . . ."

McLean had already spotted them. The well-dressed salesman trailed after him dubiously. It was like invading a private club uninvited, McLean thought with a trace of humor as he disappeared into the fitting area.

There were cubicles on both sides of a narrow aisle, discreet signs announcing that store policy dictated that these rooms might be under observation. *Observe*, McLean thought. *You may get an eyeful this time.*

He went quickly past three doors, four, before he chose one of the cubicles on his left and slipped inside, letting the half-door close quietly.

He stopped with his back pressed flat against the wall, the door to his right, a full-length mirror facing him on the opposite wall of the dressing room. He wondered if the salesman still hovered at the entrance to the fitting rooms. If Coffey had spotted him entering the Men's Store. If this was the confrontation he had avoided for the past three years. To what end? So as not to rock the boat, he thought, struck by the irony. For the good of the service. *For your country*, Zeller had said three years ago, without apology.

He kept his breathing shallow, noiseless. Only his heart threatened the quiet. The blood pounded in his ears. His hand reached under his jacket and emerged with the Colt Cobra, sliding it smoothly and silently from the oiled leather holster.

He didn't want a gun battle at Wanamaker's on a Saturday afternoon. Mental headlines leaped at him: BLOOD BATH AT WANAMAKER'S. AGENTS IN SHOOTOUT. What was it Zeller had said? *The Agency doesn't need an O.K. Corral just now.* Well, Zeller hadn't been willing to do whatever was necessary to stop Coffey. Now . . .

Someone entered the fitting rooms. McLean had heard the faint whisper of static from footsteps on the carpet. He waited, holding his breath. A customer?

A cubicle door opened, thumped shut. After a brief pause another door opened and swung closed. Another footstep brushed carpet. Another door's hinges creaked.

Not a customer, McLean thought. The row of cubicles had all been empty when he passed by.

He stared into the mirror facing him inside the small cubicle. By edging to his left, he was able to get an angle of view peering back along the corridor outside his cubicle. The door was of shoulder height and cleared the floor by about a foot. Looking into the mirror, McLean saw a pair of large brown leather shoes with thick crepe soles. The shoes were motionless a few inches beyond his cubicle door.

He waited for the shoes to move. Everything began with the feet.

The fitting rooms were absolutely still. No rustle of clothing being tried on. Nobody even breathed aloud. What were the salesmen on the floor thinking and doing? Had Coffey waved his badge at them?

The nearer shoe moved. It triggered McLean's reaction. He slammed the door outward into the advancing figure just as Coffey stepped toward it. That accident of timing doubled the force of the collision. The impact staggered Coffey.

Then McLean was through the doorway. Coffey tried to stumble clear. McLean chopped down with the barrel of the Colt. The barrel thudded against Coffey's skull. As he sagged, McLean brought his knee up hard into Coffey's groin.

The tall man seemed to fold in sections to the floor. McLean kicked Coffey's gun far along the aisle. Then he stepped over the fallen man. He left Coffey writhing on the floor in pain, sucking eggs.

McLean walked briskly through the men's department, aware of a half-dozen pairs of eyes staring at him, a few mouths gaping open. "Sorry, not quite right for me," he said to the salesman who had trailed after him.

At the top of the long escalator that dropped past the mezzanine to the main floor, he glanced back over his shoulder, sorting out the risk. Coffey would not stay down for long.

He didn't hesitate. By chance the escalator was not crowded at that moment. He went down two and three steps at a time. A moment later he strode past a carved stone eagle and through the perfumed aisles of the cosmetics department. A sign well ahead of him announced Market Street.

He saw Stacy Barrett on the sidewalk before he saw Angie. Stacy's eyes widened as she recognized him. Her head snapped around and she said something to someone behind the wheel of a white Oldsmobile Cutlass coupe.

Then McLean was running toward them, eyes only for Angie. Stacy Barrett cried, "My God, I thought you were—"

McLean pushed past her and slid onto the seat beside Angie. He grinned at her foolishly. "I thought you'd never get here," he said. "Let's go—fast!"

16

Angie stood at the window with her back to him, dark and slender and oddly vulnerable. Since they had shut the door to the apartment, closing themselves off from the world outside, she had seemed shy, uncertain with him. "Stacy's husband owns this building," she said. "We can stay here as long as we like. It's safe."

"What about Tony?"

His name made her face light up. "He's fine. He's with Stacy's mother, along with Brent—that's Stacy's son. They're the same age and they get along great."

He couldn't take his eyes off her. She was more vivid, more alive than the woman he had fallen in love with. That had been Angie too, but an Angie under wraps. Now she was released. It was as if he had seen her only in black-and-white before, he thought; now she was in vivid Technicolor.

The apartment was in a renovated old building near the waterfront west of the Benjamin Franklin Bridge. The unit was on the eighth floor. From the window in the living room where she stood, and the small balcony outside, there was a spectacular view of the span of the bridge vaulting over the Delaware River. There were a number of similar old buildings in the area, many of them abandoned warehouses or manufacturing sites that were either being torn down to make way for high-rise apartments and condominiums or renovated to create the same.

"We should have talked more than we did," Angie said quietly. "We had a lot in common. I guess we should have trusted each other."

"With our secrets?" He paused a moment. "We'd both learned you can't always trust."

"Even so . . ."

"Trust takes practice," McLean said. "It's something you have to work at. You don't just fall into it one morning."

He crossed the room to stand behind her, following her gaze toward the bridge. The late afternoon sun lit a line of fire along the curving span.

When he touched her shoulders, she flinched. "I'm sorry," she said quickly. "I can't forget that man shooting at you at Wanamaker's."

"I'd never have put you at risk if I'd known he was there."

"How did he find you?"

McLean shrugged. "He's good at it. He must have followed Stacy, hoping that she would lead him either to you or to me."

She turned toward him, startled. "Why to me?"

McLean met her anxious gaze without wavering. No more secrets, he thought; no more holding back. "He knew about you, and that I was trying to find you. If he couldn't track me down, getting to me through Stacy and you was the next best thing. All he had to do was watch Stacy and wait for you or me to show up."

Angie shivered. "What kind of world do you live in?"

"The same one you live in," he answered gently. "There are vicious people in it. Most people aren't . . . but some are."

"That's not telling the whole truth."

"There'll be time enough for that."

"I think I need to know."

He was silent for a long time. He moved away from her, as if to seek the camouflage of the borrowed room. When he came back he took her again by the shoulders and asked, "First? You need to know first?"

Her lips parted, the frown deepened, a crease between her eyebrows. Then, like the sun emerging from behind a cloud, her expression cleared. Her mouth softened into an open smile. "You came for me. That's really everything, isn't it?"

She was even more beautiful than the image he always carried of her in his mind. Her skin was honey, the same sweetness was on her lips. They made love slowly, both anxious to recapture every sensation they had believed lost. Peeled clothes away as if in slow motion. Felt each other's flesh. Explored soft mouths, let limbs entwine naturally.

When he entered her slowly, he felt a different quivering begin within her, not fear this time but spasms of pleasure and joy.

They lay motionless for a long time in each other's arms. Through the window they could see the lights of the bridge curving against the evening sky. "Tell me about Louis," he said.

"He changed. I think the dope had a lot to do with it. He wasn't only a seller, he was a user. He began by experimenting and he found that he loved it. It . . . released something in him." She paused to examine the thought. "I don't mean that cocaine made him what he is."

"He's an essentially evil man—there are such—with a veneer of civilization," suggested McLean. "The dope removed that veneer. What was left was the elemental man."

"Yes . . . it might have been like that." Angie hesitated, searching for the right words to say what she had to say. "In the beginning he was nice. Handsome and charming and attentive— he can be like that when he wants. We had some good times. What did I have to complain of?" The question was edged with bitterness. "There I was with my very own Italian stallion. Envy of the neighborhood."

"I'm not sure I want to hear this," he said as lightly as he could manage.

"Oh!" She seemed startled that he had misunderstood. "He never made love to me. He only banged a broad. Do you understand what I'm saying?"

"I think so. I hope so."

They were both silent. Lights crept along the bridge, other souls finding hope in the darkness. After a while he said, "Dope isn't the only way to release that kind of evil."

"What else could possibly make a man like that?"

"Different kinds of excitement," he said slowly. "Different highs. Power, for instance."

She studied him closely, her eyes huge. "You're talking about *your* enemies, not mine."

"Yes. Some men in my line of work become obsessed with their mission. And seduced by the knowledge that they can be a power unto themselves. Self-righteousness combined with power . . . it's as dangerous as any drug."

"I guess it's time for you to tell me about those scars," she said, a fingertip gently tracing some of the hard ridges across his skin.

"They go with the territory."

"Being a spy?"

"Yes."

"You know about me and Louis," she whispered. "Tell me why that man at Wanamaker's was trying to kill you."

It seemed as good a time and place as there would ever be to begin their long knowing of each other. She needed to know who and what he was, as he was discovering her. They could talk in the darkness of the room, and their stories seemed somehow detached from them, these languid lovers in their rumpled bed.

"He thinks I killed his best friend," said McLean.

"Did you?"

"Yes."

"In the late sixties and early seventies I was a field agent, first in Vietnam and later in Africa. Then, at the beginning of the eighties, I was brought in from the field. That was mostly because the Agency was beginning to concentrate more and more on remote analysis. Most of our Estimates, as they're called, of what is happening or about to happen in the world that will affect our country are based today on technological surveillance methods rather than on human resources." He smiled faintly at the term. "Whether for better or worse, the Agency was emasculated by the attacks against it in the seventies. That's one reason things were so difficult in Iran, for instance, when the Iranians took over our embassy in Tehran and held all of our hostages for so long. We didn't *have* human resources in Iran who could give us the on-site information needed. We had to rely on others—the British and Canadians, for instance, were able to do more than we could.

"Anyway, I became an analyst. And I was put on the African desk because I'd served there in the field." He was silent for a while, thinking of the irony that after so many years it was surprisingly difficult to *reveal* secrets. "The Third World nations of Africa have been pawns in one tug of war after another for a long time. Between the Soviets and us. Between white Africans and blacks. The administration's position on South Africa during President Reagan's two terms was ambiguous, to say the least. A little nudging toward relaxation of apartheid, but not enough to upset the South Africans—or to cause them to make any drastic changes.

"Carl Warner was one of our agents in Udombo, one of those emerging small nations on the South African border. He was one of the Agency's heroes, going way back . . . the Cold War in Europe, Vietnam, Cuba, Chile, El Salvador, wherever the Agency has had a major impact in the last thirty years. I trained under him. Admired him, even though he had a one-track mind as far as the Soviets go. He thought anyone who wanted to give the Russians the benefit of the doubt on anything was thinking at kindergarten level." He looked at Angie closely. "That doesn't mean I didn't respect him, or back him up when he was carrying out assignments. That was his job, and mine.

"So when I started to see something funny going on, some things that didn't add up right, on the South African border with one of its smaller Third World neighbors where Warner was operating, at first I didn't want to believe what I was seeing. But I had to go on looking, and the pattern began to be unmistakable.

"Warner's job was to try to get two rival factions in Udombo to resolve their differences. Their conflict was really rooted in ancient tribal rivalry, the kind that makes democratic governments so shaky all over Africa, and no amount of talking was going to erase centuries of hostility. The second part of Warner's job was to keep the more radical of the two groups, which had Marxist elements, from making trouble for South Africa.

"We had a fairly modest aid package going to Udombo, and

Warner also had a lot to say about how the money was to be allocated. It was supposed to be for humanitarian needs, no weapons. I started getting feedback from here and there that armed clashes were increasing between the two main rival tribes, not decreasing. And that one—the radical, leftist-influenced group—was making raids across the border into South Africa."

"Exactly what wasn't supposed to be happening," Angie murmured.

"Exactly. What came next was predictable. I reported as much to my superior, a man named Zeller, a deputy director of operations. Two weeks later it happened, just as I'd predicted. South Africa struck back hard across the border into Udombo, wiping out one whole village, killing scores of people, and using the strike as an excuse for a scorched-earth trample through the area before pulling back."

Angie appeared puzzled. "Okay, analyst, I give up. What was going on?"

"Someone was deliberately escalating things. Setting the tribes against each other, encouraging raids, giving the South Africans an excuse to cross the border . . . and then waiting for the backlash."

"But no one would . . ."

"Someone did. The radical tribe won all kinds of converts after the South African attack. If they had the weapons to hit back, it was a foregone conclusion they would. Probably they would have done it even if they had to use sticks and knives. All they needed was a leader. When we began to get rumors they had one, a white man, urgent instructions went to our man in the field—Warner—to try to put a damper on things until tempers cooled.

"About this same time, by accident I stumbled on an unrelated report of some arms sales. A former agent was involved. He was monitored. The arms supposedly went to Libya, in violation of the law, and the agent was arrested at Kennedy trying to leave the country.

"But the arms had disappeared."

Angie shivered as if with cold. She hugged herself with her arms, but when he asked if she was cold she shook her head. She walked over to the sofa, which faced the view window of the living room, and sat in it, still hugging her chest. McLean sat beside her, and for a time they were silent, looking out at the deepening darkness, the lights across the bridge, a fragment of Philadelphia's skyline.

"You put a lot of little pieces together," McLean said. "A report about a couple of leaders of the more moderate black party in Udombo being assassinated. A South African complaint that Udomban rebels were seen with modern weapons. A bloody clash between the rival factions, with one side—the moderates—badly outmanned and outgunned. A report from another service—the British—about an American seen in Somersberg, a town in South Africa near the Udomban border, coming out of a hotel where a colonel in command of the South African army division in the area was staying.

"I put all the pieces together the way I saw them fitting and bucked my Estimate up to Zeller, the man I mentioned. A week later he called me in. He was sitting there with my report on his desk, looking like thunder. As if he wanted to trash the report and me, there and then."

"But he didn't," Angie said. It was not a question.

"He didn't because he could see what I saw. He's not what you'd call an emotional man, is Zeller," McLean said with a wry smile. "He doesn't get wrapped up in myths or personalities. He saw what Carl Warner was doing as clearly as I did."

"Warner!"

"He was arming the rebels, the radical tribe. That gave them immediate superiority over the moderates, which you would think, given Warner's right-wing views, was just what he didn't want. The radicals were starting a program of genocide, the kind of bloodbath that can't be stopped once it gets started, given the past history of tribal warfare. He was also training those rebels, encouraging them, whipping up their anger and hatred, pointing them at South Africa."

"He'd sided with the radicals in spite of his own views," Angie said. "In some ways you can't blame him."

"That's what people were supposed to think. It's what most people in the Agency thought afterwards. Warner looked like one of the good guys. For once, our man in the field wasn't siding with the heavies, he was in there with the downtrodden who were fighting for their freedom and dignity."

"But . . . wasn't he?"

"Oh, sure he was. A devious man, our Warner. He knew exactly what he was leading them into."

"I'm not sure . . ." Angie's eyes suddenly widened as she remembered. "You said you killed him."

McLean didn't respond immediately. He rose from the couch and went to the window once more to stare at the far horizon. "Zeller sent me down there. A secret mission—he always plays things close to the vest. I'd been a field agent there, I knew Africa, I knew Warner, I was one of the very few privy to what Warner was up to. Maybe the only one besides Zeller himself. So nobody knew I was going in. Nobody knew later why I was there." He swung around to peer at her face, which caught highlights from the window. The room remained in darkness. "The White House didn't want bad headlines out of Africa. They didn't want a bloodbath, and especially not one where one of our agents was involved. They didn't want to give Johannesburg license to go into a struggling little country on its border in force . . . which turned out to be what the South Africans were planning."

Angie shook her head, not so much in bewilderment as in resistance to the story he was relating.

"Warner was playing his own game," said McLean. "If you'd taken a vote at the time, maybe half the people in the Agency would have applauded him for it. The hard-liners, the real Cold Warriors. Warner was arming the radical Marxists, all right, but he hadn't swung left himself. He was manipulating them. Playing on their naiveté and their black nationalism. Lining them up and sending them out to be massacred. The way Warner had planned it, when it was over the radical group would have been destroyed, the South Africans would have some welcome breathing space, and the moderates in Udombo—what was left of them—would be able to pick up the pieces."

"My God!" Angie exclaimed, the horror of the plot bursting on her. She shook her head sharply again, a shocked refusal to accept what she was hearing. Reacting with the same incredulity most observers had felt, McLean thought, even in the Agency.

"You were sent to . . . to stop him."

"I got there too late," McLean said with bitterness. "I came in through South Africa, the way Zeller had it set up. I was near the border when the Udombans crossed over. They marched straight into a trap. The South African army had been alerted, and they were waiting for the invaders.

"I went across the border trying to find Warner. He had disappeared just before the fighting started. It took me five days, but I finally found him in Somersberg, back across the border in South Africa." McLean paused. "He laughed at me. He'd accomplished everything he set out to do. He had no apologies."

"And you . . . killed him?"

McLean shook his head emphatically. "I told him I was going to see that the whole story got out, including the part he'd played in setting it up, even if I had to resign from the Agency. He went berserk and came after me. In the fighting . . . his own gun went off." In the long silence that followed, the echo of that gunshot seemed to reverberate in the dark room. "I'd been careful. Nobody had seen me enter the hotel. Warner was found in his room, his own gun in his hand, his prints the only ones on it. It looked like suicide. He'd led the Udombans into a disaster, blamed himself, and taken his own life.

"That's the way it read. The White House wasn't too happy about the flareup, but we had scored some points in the Third World because of it. The Marxists had been decimated, which made the President happy. The South Africans were happy with the outcome. Our man ended up looking like one of the good guys even though his troops were slaughtered."

"But if that was the end of it . . ."

"It wasn't." McLean shrugged, as if happy endings were never to be expected. "Someone stumbled on the fact that I'd been in the vicinity. Some of Warner's friends started asking questions. I was placed in Somersberg. There was skepticism about Warner ever committing suicide. He wasn't the type." McLean gave a long sigh, as if telling the story had exhausted him. As if he were shedding a burden of guilt or remorse in the telling. He rejoined Angie on the couch, and she put a hand on his knee, resting it there. "He was an Agency hero. It looked as if I'd had something to do with his death. But Zeller didn't want the truth to come out. Not because of Warner. Because it would make the Agency look bad. And the administration didn't want to change the story. Neither did the South Africans."

"And you?" Angie asked quietly. "What did you want?"

McLean took his time answering. He had thought about it a lot over the past three years. The answer always came out the same. "The Agency was my life," he said. "I believed in it, in spite of some of the glitches. Coming at that time, the story of what Carl Warner had done would have been exactly what the Agency's critics and enemies wanted. It would have destroyed the Agency, even though it had acted properly as an organization. Carl Warner did what he did on his own—not the first time that's happened with some of the Cold Warriors. They have their own force within the Agency. But the incident would have been seen simply as one of our agents setting up the black Africans for a massacre, while we played footsie with the South Africans. It would have harmed not only the Agency but the country, at home and especially with the Third World countries."

McLean met her troubled gaze. "That's why I agreed to retire. Some of Warner's friends convinced themselves that I had something to do with his death. They made a couple of tries at me, so Zeller arranged for me to disappear, the way you were given a new identity and stashed out there in Fortune."

"The man at Wanamaker's is one of Warner's friends."

McLean nodded. "I think the only one still hunting me. He was always one of the Agency's cowboys, and close to Carl Warner. Nobody can stop him . . ."

"Is he crazy?" Angie was appalled and frightened. Cowboys and gun battles were something for the television screen, not for the glossy aisles of John Wanamaker's department store. "Why can't they stop him?"

"He doesn't think of himself as crazy. He's avenging a fallen angel. He's out of control, and I guess you'd have to say that's not quite sane. As for the Agency stopping him . . ." McLean paused, examining what he was about to say. "I'm not sure they want to."

He smiled as the dismay in her eyes shaded rapidly into anger. "Is it Zeller, still? What kind of man is he?"

"He's not encouraging Coffey. It's just that I'm a problem Zeller wishes would go away. He won't be too upset if something happens to me."

* * *

They made love again, as a kind of mutual reassurance, holding a dangerous world at bay.

Afterward she said, "I didn't really know you before. I wondered if we would like each other. I was afraid . . . it might not work if we took off the masks."

"And now?"

"I love you."

"I've always secretly loved you."

Toward midnight, as they lay drowsily in each other's arms, the phone rang. Angie let it ring on and on, reluctant to answer it. "One of us better," McLean said at last. "Who knows we're here?"

"Only Stacy."

She fumbled for the telephone on the night table beside the bed. Held it so McLean could hear the voice on the line.

Hear Stacy Barrett sobbing, crying aloud, "Tony's gone!"

17

THE GRAND OLD RANDALL HOUSE on Chestnut Hill dated back to the early 1900s. It was of red brick, three stories high with full columns supporting a wide front porch. A huge greenhouse was attached to the south wall. The house was set amidst companionable estates in the northwest corner of Philadelphia. The parklike grounds were overlaid by tall old cedar and elm trees, their branches woven into a shade so dense that the deep shadows below seemed to swallow up the lights along the drive from the gates.

No alarm system, McLean was reminded as he drove in. The padlock and chain on the wrought iron gates set into the perimeter wall had been cut through with heavy metal cutters. The shadows made surreptitious approach to the house easy—once the guard dog had been disposed of.

Stacy Barrett's mother, a Randall, was a woman in her sixties with gray hair crowning patrician features. She was in bed, her

doctor soberly on hand to caution against further questioning.
A burly policeman was in the great entry hall when McLean and
Angie arrived. He glanced at McLean suspiciously, then turned
his attention to Angie's legs as she raced up the winding staircase
after Stacy.

"The boy's mother?" the cop asked McLean.

"That's right."

"I'm Turner, Sergeant." He said it as if sergeant were a
Christian name. "You family?"

"A friend. Barney McLean."

"A friend, huh." Turner seemed to regard this as highly
suspicious. "These people." His gaze took in the entry hall with
its oak staircase, the huge crystal chandelier that shed its sparkle
over the stairs and the polished oak floors below, the shadowed
rooms off the hall, the Oriental rugs underfoot, as if these things
defined what kind of people he was talking about. "What it looks
like, the boy's father came and took him. Don't matter how loud
you yell about kidnapping, that's not what it is."

"If he took the boy, it was against his will."

"Yeah?" The cop shrugged. "Who's to say? What is the kid,
three years old? Point is, the parents are still married, from what
I'm told. The mother was hiding the boy from his father. I'm not
saying who's right or wrong, who's good or bad. Only that it's
no kidnapping, not in the eyes of the law."

McLean thought Turner talked more freely than most cops.
He said, "The father's name is Louis Marchetti."

If the name meant anything to Turner, he didn't show it by
so much as a blink. The speculative eyes in the beefy face
seemed more interested in who McLean was and what he was
doing here . . . but not too interested in that either.

"The boy and his mother have been under the government's
Witness Protection Program," said McLean. "Protected from the
father."

"Yeah?" The cop gazed around the elegant entry hall once more. A broad shoe nosed into the deep pile of a Persian rug. "I didn't know they had any safe houses like this. Hell, maybe I could get into the program myself."

"Does that mean you're not going to do anything about it?"

The cop studied McLean for a long minute. He looked as if he were nostalgic for the good old days of rubber hoses and private, soundproofed cells. "We'll look into it, McLean. But until somebody shows me different, there's no crime. It's a domestic quarrel. If the government thinks different, maybe you should give them a call."

"Maybe I will."

Sergeant Turner left a few minutes later, burdened only by regret that he had no real excuse to take McLean along with him. Philly's finest, McLean reflected, didn't necessarily mean the friendliest.

The council of war was held over coffee the following morning in the library, a huge walnut-paneled room whose walls held shelves of books reaching so high that a sliding ladder was in place along the main wall to provide access to the upper shelves. There was a big leaded-glass bay window with a window seat, a couple of other tall casement windows, a fireplace big enough to drive through, wall niches holding framed prints of sailing ships and, over the wooden mantel, a portrait of a handsome silver-haired woman with the same violet eyes Stacy Barrett had. McLean took her to be Stacy's mother.

"You talked to the other boy?" McLean asked Stacy.

She nodded. "He was asleep when it happened. He heard nothing, saw nothing." She sensed McLean's next question and added, "Tony was in his own room. There are plenty of rooms." A slight wave of her hand hinted at endless corridors.

Besides Angie, McLean, and Stacy Barrett, there were two surprising presences in the room, Brad Randall and Freddy Mills. The two young men had trouble meeting McLean's eyes. They mumbled half-swallowed apologies while at the same time appearing as resolute as they had when McLean was seen as the enemy. Now, it seemed, they were equally determined to make amends by helping to get Tony back. "He's a good kid," Brad Randall said. Freddy set his massive jaws with unspoken determination.

"We should have anticipated something like this," Stacy said. "But I never dreamed Louis would find Tony here with Mother."

"No point in blaming yourself," said McLean. "It's done. Louis would have found him sooner or later no matter where he stayed." He glanced at Angie, reading in her white-faced silence the cost of holding herself under control. "He found you both in California, even if it took him three years. Philadelphia is his territory."

"He's not going to keep him," Angie said.

"No . . . he's not."

"I think you should see my lawyer," Stacy said. "I'm sure he will come over here today if I ask him, even though it's Sunday. Louis can't keep Tony, not with the court order still in effect. It's just going to take a little time. A few weeks, perhaps . . ."

Angie's eyes flashed. "There isn't time! I don't trust him with Tony—not for a few weeks, not even for a day." Her gaze met McLean's with an unvoiced challenge. "We can't wait."

"No," said McLean. "I'm going after him tonight."

There was a babble of reaction, Stacy Barrett quickly protesting, her brother and Freddy jumping in to say they wanted to come along, Angie watching McLean in silence, waiting for the others to quiet down before she said calmly, "I'm coming with you."

McLean shook his head. "It would be better if—"

"He's my son."

McLean studied her for a long moment, the familiar softness of her mouth now set in a firm line of defiance. He felt a tug of admiration along with the desire to take her in his arms. "That's it, then. I'm not sure about Brad and Freddy coming along. There may be trouble . . ."

"Hey, man, we'd like to help," Brad Randall insisted.

McLean hesitated only briefly before he nodded, a half-formed thought suggesting how the two muscular young men might prove useful. "Just one rule," McLean said. "This goes for everyone. I'm in charge. I don't know what we're going to run into, but we can't be going in four different directions. Understood?"

Brad and Freddy nodded eagerly. Angie was a little slower to respond, but her grudging agreement finally came, accompanied by a faint smile. "Agreed," she said.

McLean smiled back. This Angie was less pliant than the one he had been living with. But even more interesting. "Okay, you've lived in that house, you should know it pretty well. Has anyone else been there?"

Both Stacy Barrett and her brother had visited Angie in the early days of her marriage in the country house where Louis Marchetti now lived. No one had any doubt that that was where he would have taken Tony. "He knows I won't take this lying down," Angie said. "He *wants* me to come there."

"So he'll be expecting us. Or someone. That's why I need to know everything I can about the place. How to get there, the access roads, what kind of cover there might be, the nature of the terrain, all of that. And the grounds—gates, fences, outbuildings, gardens, trees, anything you can remember. After that I'll need a layout of the house. Make a sketch showing doors and windows, porches and terraces. Angie, you start on the house. Brad can do the general layout of the grounds and you can fill him in on details. I've got to make a couple of phone calls."

"When do we go?" Freddy rumbled.

"As soon as it's dark."

"You found them?" Old Tony cut straight through McLean's greeting.

"I was a little late."

Silence. Heavy, prolonged. The kind of silence that became more uncomfortable the longer it lasted. "Say what you mean," the old man rasped.

"I'm with Angie now. She's fine. She's . . . beautiful. But Tony's gone."

"Whatta ya mean, gone?"

"Kidnapped," McLean said bluntly. Old Tony would not appreciate sugar-coating. "He was staying with friends of Angie's here in Philadelphia since last week. It seemed safe—Louis wasn't supposed to know he was here."

"Louis may be stupid, but you shouldn't underestimate him."

"He found out where Tony was."

"You seem goddamn sure of Louis."

"Nobody else had reason to snatch the boy. Besides, he left a calling card."

"Yeah?" Old Tony was wheezing now. "What kind of card?"

"Young Tony was staying with the mother of one of Angie's best friends. Stacy Barrett was maid-of-honor at Angie's wedding. Maybe you remember her."

"I remember. Society broad. A looker. Also a troublemaker."

McLean didn't deny the assessment, which had been confirmed by his own experience, though he suspected that Old Tony's view was colored more by Stacy Barrett's independence than by any trouble she might have visited on the Marchetti family.

"Tony was with Stacy's son—they're good friends."

"So?"

"The place where they were staying—Stacy's mother's place—is on Chestnut Hill. It's fenced, and there was a guard dog outside at night, a Doberman."

Old Tony waited. News of violence and disaster were not strangers to him. Still, McLean could hear the labored asthmatic breathing over the phone. He wondered if, in the Mafia don's younger days as hood, extortionist, and enforcer, that wheeze had been a terrifying sound at times of stress to potential victims. Now, he thought, it was the rattle of anxiety.

"The dog was killed. Poisoned meat. Then he was nailed to a porch column near the front door of the house. When he was found, one of his eyes had been gouged out and there was something else jammed into the socket."

Leaving the picture unfinished, McLean forced the old man to ask the question. "Stop stroking me, McLean. What was the message?"

"A wedding band."

Silence again. McLean thought of the genteel lady whose life had been so far removed from anything sinister, who had found Tony missing and, opening her front door, beheld the horror of Louis Marchetti's twisted sense of humor. Little wonder that she was under a doctor's care tonight.

"The boy was gone?" Old Tony was no longer skeptical. The message was unmistakably from Louis to Angie.

"No one heard anything. There are locks on the doors but no alarm system. A padlock on the gates was cut and a door to the house was pried open. Young Tony was taken. He might have gone with his father without a fuss. Would that be true?"

"Why not? Every kid knows his father."

"Angie tells me Louis has a house out in Montgomery County where they lived during the first two years of her marriage. Does Louis stay there now?"

"Yeah. Nice place in the country," Old Tony said. "Too goddamn quiet."

"I'm going after the boy," said McLean. "I thought you should know."

"You want my blessing?" the old man asked angrily.

"You know better."

"Yeah." How far would the old man go to save his grandson? How strong was the tie of loyalty to his son? McLean knew that Old Tony's conflicting emotions might tip him either way.

But when the answer came it was not emotion speaking but cold reason. Business. Louis Marchetti had stepped over the line. He had broken the rules before—in setting up his own drug network, in abusing his wife and child, in defying the organization. He had gotten away with it, almost certainly because of the respect owed to his father. Now Louis had gone a step further. He was an embarrassment. He was also out of control, and that made him even more of a liability.

"What do you want, McLean?"

"I figure Louis has bodyguards around the place. I wondered if maybe they didn't also work for you."

Silence. If Old Tony chose to, he could alert the bodyguards and make McLean's attempt to break in doubly difficult and dangerous, if not impossible.

"You want them gone."

"Yes."

"You're goin' after the boy yourself?"

"Angie and me."

"Angie? You're lettin' her go in there?" Old Tony was dumbfounded.

"I can't stop her."

The silence did not last as long this time. The wheezing had become even more audible. "Louis has one man, close to him, his name is Richie. Works for Louis himself. The outdoor people, that's another story." Old Tony paused. "When are you goin' in?"

"Tonight after dark."

"The outdoor people I know. They won't bother you. If I tried to get to Richie, Louis would hear."

"I understand. I just wanted you to know . . . it's not personal."

"Yeah."

"The boy should be with his mother, not with Louis. Louis will destroy him."

"You haven't got him back yet." For a moment Old Tony Marchetti spoke as if he still wanted to believe in his son's prowess.

"You won't interfere?"

"After tonight," the old man said, "it would be best if I never saw you or heard from you again. You understand?"

"I understand."

"It's between you and Louis."

"That's all I want."

"Watch out for Richie," Old Tony said.

There was a last deep rattle from his throat before the line went dead. It was like the sound of someone dying.

Telephones were such anonymous instruments of communication. Breaking up a relationship by phone, McLean thought, would be an act both cruel and cowardly. Exposing an act of betrayal in the same impersonal way made a bloodless action out of something that should have been angry and painful.

McLean tried to reach Eric Zeller through Langley. Zeller

was not available but McLean's message was recorded. Then he called Paul Thornton at his home in Tyson's Corners. The call triggered an answering device. McLean listened to Jane Thornton's cheerful assurance that, though neither she nor Paul was available to come to the phone just now, if he would leave his name and the time he called one of them would be glad to get back to him as soon as possible.

When the beep sounded McLean said, "It's me again, Paul. I need to talk to Zeller as soon as possible. It's urgent—"

"Barney? Sorry about the answering machine, I was out in the yard." The recording was cut off as Paul Thornton picked up the phone. "Where are you? What's happening?"

"I'm in Philadelphia," McLean said, thinking that Paul's apology had been too quick. Had he waited to hear who was calling? He gave Thornton a brief rundown of his search for Angie, leaving out the attack in Riverton but including Clark Coffey's attack in the John Wanamaker store. "It wasn't exactly a shootout, Paul, but the next thing to it."

"Oh my God!" Thornton's distress seemed genuine. "Zeller will go through the roof."

"Where is he? Can you reach him today?"

"No . . . no, it's impossible. Not because it's Sunday. He's on another case, Barney—hell, there's a lot going on besides your situation. Zeller's out of town, that's all I know. Listen, I'll do what I can. Where can I reach you?"

McLean read the phone number off the telephone, then added, "I'm not sure how long I'll be here. Tell Zeller that Louis Marchetti has taken Tony. I'm going to get him back."

"That's crazy, Barney! There are legal steps—"

"Not good enough, Paul. It's something I have to do. We think Marchetti is holding the boy at his home out in Montgomery County. I'll wait until tonight but no longer. Then I'm going there to bring the boy back."

"You're sure you won't reconsider this, Barney? Zeller won't like it, you know that. And Marchetti could be dangerous."

"It's not Zeller's decision." McLean was silent a moment before he said, "I don't work for him any more."

When the call to Thornton was completed, McLean thought about what he had said and left unsaid. He felt a weight of depression, sensing an end to many things of which he had been reluctant to let go.

The weight lifted when Angie came into the room. She walked straight into his arms, and he held her for a long time in silence.

18

THE DAY PASSED. Angie sketched the house and grounds. Brad
and Freddy went off to find the supplies McLean had asked for.
Stacy Barrett spent time with her son, trying to quiet his fears.
Stacy's mother recovered sufficiently to dismiss her doctor and
order some grilled mushrooms on toast for lunch.

The police did not return.

Gradually the house where Louis Marchetti had almost certainly taken young Tony took shape in McLean's mind. The land
was rolling and wooded. The house itself stood in the open at
the top of a knoll. Its core, a gray stone Georgian of symmetrical
proportions, dated back to 1825. Succeeding generations of
owners had added onto it with some care for the original architec-
ture, principally in identical east and west wings framing the
original house. Contemptuous of tradition, Louis Marchetti had
himself designed a huge, modern "entertainment" room jutting
out from the south face of the main house, with walls of glass

overlooking an Olympic-sized swimming pool. "I don't know what other changes he might have made," Angie concluded. "It's been three years."

"Are there any other buildings?"

"The garage is under the east wing. There are the original stables, but they're empty." She made an attempt at a smile. "Louis likes to bet on horses, not ride them."

"Anything else?"

"Well . . . I remember a tool shed. And the gate house, of course, but that's a long way from the house. Here . . . see it on the diagram?"

"How far?"

"Oh . . . a quarter mile?"

McLean studied the layout. "What's this?" Where a stream cut across the west corner of the property, along its bank Angie had drawn a box indicating another structure.

"Oh, that's the old mill."

"A mill?"

"It was a functioning mill for over a century, serving the farmers around here, and it still works. Or at least it did when I was there. The people who owned the house last used to grind a little wheat, not commercially but just as a hobby. There's a big water wheel at the bottom level, and everything works off that, with great big gears and shafts and pulleys and all. It even has its own little elevators to carry the grain up or down. The building has about five levels."

She paused, her gaze distant, and McLean thought she had liked the old mill. A place to explore and touch the past and fantasize with a small boy. Tony had been too young to appreciate it then, only a year old . . .

"Take me over the grounds," said McLean.

* * *

The group assembled late in the afternoon in the paneled library of the house on Chestnut Hill. Stacy Barrett didn't much care for the way McLean had taken charge that day. She was also, she said, worried about Brad and Freddy. "I don't really like this, Angie. I don't think the boys should be involved."

"Aw, Stace, get off my back!" Brad protested.

"Sounds like fun to me," Freddy the Giant said. He was looking forward to using his battering-ram pickup. He liked it so much, he said, that he was thinking about keeping the front end that way, with a massive six-by-twelve-inch plank of wood mounted to the front bumper as McLean had directed.

"It's not a fun caper," said McLean. "And you guys won't be getting out of that truck."

"Hey, man—!"

"You're the rescue team. When we find the boy, it's your job to get him and Angie out of there fast. Give me the diversion I need at the start, and then be ready for the pickup. That's all you have to do. And that's plenty, believe me."

"But—"

"There's only one chief in this war party, right?"

The young men reluctantly agreed, and Stacy Barrett's protests were also overridden.

"Is there, like, anything else we can do?" Brad asked.

"Ask your sister if she could whip up something to eat," McLean said with a smile at Stacy. "Not mushrooms on toast."

Having been offered the opportunity to display her take-charge efficiency, Stacy whipped up a surprisingly delicious feast of cold chicken, salad, hot rolls, and fresh garden peas. There was little conversation during the meal. Everyone's thoughts were occupied with what lay ahead.

Over coffee McLean gazed out of the window at a sky turning ominously black. "Do you have one of those phone numbers that gives weather updates?"

"Yeah, sure, man." Brad remained eager to help.

"Check the weather forecast."

Brad came back in a few minutes with a long face. "Rain!" he blurted. "There's a storm moving in." In the same instant he seemed to remember the last time he had confronted McLean in the eye of a storm, and a flush dyed his cheeks. "Is that bad?"

McLean raised his coffee cup toward the others in a kind of toast. His eyes met Angie's and he smiled. "It couldn't be better."

The storm broke in the early evening, bringing premature darkness. The two cars—Brad and Freddy in the latter's modified Datsun pickup, Angie and McLean following in the white Oldsmobile convertible that was leased to Rod Barrett's investment firm—drove north amidst earth-jarring thunderclaps and bolts of lightning that lit up the countryside like flashing film clips.

There was little traffic for a Sunday evening. McLean and Angie rode in silence, Angie at the wheel because of her familiarity with the route and their destination. Although the storm walled them in, its fury made conversation difficult.

Earlier lovemaking a distant memory, McLean felt Angie's remoteness. It was her past they were driving toward, he thought. Her shattered dream of love and marriage. Her son . . .

"You love him too." Angie seemed to divine his thoughts.

"Very much."

"We'll bring him back."

"Yes."

"You haven't told me everything . . ."

"About tonight? No."

Nodding, she fell silent again. Accepting his silence. A trust was growing between them that had not been possible before. Secrets made uneasy beds.

The estate was in suburban Montgomery County. Angie and McLean became separated from the young men in the pickup at a traffic light, but McLean had anticipated the possibility. They met in Blue Bell in the parking lot of an historic inn that appeared warm and inviting on this stormy night.

Deliberately McLean went through the ritual of having Brad and Freddy match the time on their watches to his. Routine details were a way of channeling nervousness, and the two youths were clearly nervous now, eyeing each other, wondering what they had got themselves into. "You'll hit the gates at exactly nine o'clock—we'll go over the wall right after you. That doesn't mean 8:59 or 9:01, okay?"

"Sure, man . . ."

"Give us thirty minutes. That should give you time to pry yourself loose and circle the back roads. Come in the service road on the south side of the estate at nine-thirty. Then you get yourselves, Angie, and Tony out of here."

No one asked the obvious questions. What if McLean failed? What if Angie and Tony weren't there to be picked up? What if Brad and Freddy had trouble with guards at the gates?

"Ready?"

Brad swallowed. Brushing the dampness from his close-cropped hair, Freddy said, "Let's go."

The two young men climbed back into the red pickup. Its headlights moved off down the dark road, digging their own tunnel. After a moment the white Oldsmobile followed.

The center of the storm had moved eastward, and over the rich farmlands north of Philadelphia, where early settlers had once fought to shape a raw wilderness into a promising new land, the rain had settled into a steady, gentle dripping.

McLean had borrowed a dark blue jacket from Brad Randall.

Angie wore a black waist-length windbreaker of her own. A scarf around her head covered her dark hair. They had been out of the car less than a minute before they were thoroughly soaked. Once you were wet enough, McLean knew, getting wetter no longer mattered.

He checked his watch with a penlight, then eyed the stone wall surrounding Louis Marchetti's estate. The wall was about eight feet high, topped with broken glass. If there was also a perimeter alarm, McLean hoped that having Freddy's truck crash the gates would break the circuit and hide a penetration at a different point along the wall.

McLean had no illusion that this would be the only barrier. Louis Marchetti played games too dangerous to rely on minimum security.

McLean had brought along a professional painter's ladder that folded out in sections. By raising it a notch above eight feet in height, he could fold it over the wall without touching the barrier, forming a modern version of a fence-climbing stile.

A grinding crash rent the dripping peacefulness of the night. It came from about two hundred feet away, around a curve of the road, close enough for McLean to see headlights filtered through a screen of trees.

"Over you go!" he urged Angie.

They dropped from the ladder into a pine grove, damp and dark and fragrant. The ground was overlaid with a bed of old needles, soft underfoot. As McLean crouched beside Angie, another angry cry of ripping metal reached them from the gates off to their right.

No shouts, McLean thought, though these might have been smothered by the dripping rain. No gunshots either, which would not have been smothered.

McLean led the way, following the course pictured in his mind. They were in the northeast corner of the estate, moving down a long slope through a small but crowded wood. As they dodged among the trees, McLean pondered what additional alarm system Marchetti might have installed against the possibility that his outer perimeter might be penetrated. Would he have relied on guards alone for his inner security? A roving patrol?

For several minutes there had been no further sound from the direction of the gates. Did that mean that Old Tony had been as good as his word? Otherwise Brad and Freddy would be doing some fast talking.

Angie gave a small cry. She stumbled to her knees. Quickly beside her, McLean asked, "You okay? What—?"

He broke off. The rain had caused a small mound of earth to collapse into a narrow ditch, unearthing a square black box. Angie had tripped over it. With his fingers McLean carefully traced the buried wires that ran from the box underground in both directions.

"Pressure sensors," he told Angie. "They react to the weight of a human being. Lesser pressures, like the weight of small animals, won't trigger the alarm."

"Does that mean . . . Louis knows right where we are *right now*?"

"Probably."

They stopped in the shadows at the edge of the stand of pine trees. Below them, at the foot of the slope, a natural gully gushed with about a foot of water. It offered no obstacle, for the runoff was no more than a yard across. Beyond it the land rose gently toward the house on the top of the knoll. The old unused stables—now an empty shell—intervened. McLean could make out the low angular shape of the stables and the roof of the house beyond them.

"What are we waiting for?"

"To see if someone responds to the alarm."

"What about the guards at the gate?"

McLean was silent a moment before he said, "I don't think they're here tonight."

"But . . ."

"Down!" he whispered sharply.

They flattened against the soggy turf. The smells of grass and damp earth and pine needles were pungent. McLean's attention focused on the running figure that slanted across the slope from the direction of the house. Near the noisy gully at the bottom of the hill the figure paused. McLean saw the man glance toward the main gates, as if puzzled. Then he raised something to his mouth. A walkie-talkie of some sort, McLean guessed. *And he's wondering why there's no response from the other guards.*

Richie, McLean thought. Left alone . . .

The black-clad figure seemed to reach a decision. He turned away from the gates toward the wood. Someone else was supposed to be covering the gates, but an intrusion in the vicinity of the wood demanded immediate investigation.

Richie leaped lightly across the gully with its swift rush of water and angled up the slope toward the pines. His course would bring him about thirty feet to the right of the spot where McLean and Angie lay.

McLean slid his Colt automatic from its holster and held it against his chest.

Richie ran in a practiced, zigzag line, hugging the ground, presenting a poor target in the rain-streaked darkness.

At the edge of the wood he went into a crouch and stayed motionless, listening. Only his head moved—and his eyes.

McLean knew the instant Richie spotted them. They were not deep enough into the cover of the trees for their ground-hugging silhouettes to escape a hunter's sharp eyes. McLean eased his gun clear, and Richie jumped quickly toward the line of trees closest to him.

What happened next was too swift and unexpected to be immediately grasped. There was a sudden sharp cry, a whirring like wild birds taking flight, a scream of agony.

Then silence.

Angie lay trembling, staring in the direction of the blood-chilling sounds.

"Don't move," McLean said.

He crawled toward the place where Richie had entered the wood.

The first thing he saw was a natural path winding up the hill and entering the wood. Richie had followed it, trusting his knowledge of the terrain.

Someone else had anticipated his coming and the path he would follow.

The booby trap was simple and familiar. McLean had seen a dozen or more like it in Vietnam, used by the Vietnamese on both sides of that conflict. Richie, not expecting a trap on his own ground, had followed the path and stepped on or tripped over a wire. He lay half-sitting against the base of a tree, a half-dozen sharp wooden stakes driven into his belly and groin by the hidden catapult he had released. One hand clutched one of the bloody stakes.

His eyes were still open in shock and horror.

Richie was good, Old Tony had implied. Just not good enough.

When McLean returned to Angie, she said, "Who . . . who is it?"

"A man named Richie, I think. One of Louis's bodyguards."

"He's dead?"

"Yes."

She didn't ask how. That he had blundered in the darkness into some terrible kind of trap was obvious. She stared toward the tree against which Richie rested, like someone tired after a long journey, and asked, "Who did that? Somehow it's not like something Louis would do."

"No. Someone expected him—or someone like him—to respond to any alarm. There might be other booby traps as well, so we'll have to watch our own step."

Angie studied him for a long moment. "You know who did it, don't you?"

"Let's find out what's happening at the house before we jump to any conclusions."

He started down the slope without waiting for her response, forcing her to hurry after him through the curtain of rain. At the foot of the slope, from which the house was invisible, they stepped across the gully. The rise toward the stables was grassy, close-cropped and offering no cover. *You could have set it up here*, McLean thought. *Why didn't you?*

He remembered how Carl Warner had enjoyed the gamesmanship of his trade. Coffey would be the same. He didn't want this confrontation to be too crude or too quick. He wanted to play it out, to savor it. He had waited a long time . . .

Crouching at a corner of the stone-walled stables, McLean studied the big house on the top of the knoll. The house was dark except for a room at the back off to his left—the kitchen, he remembered from Angie's sketch—and the entertainment room, which projected out from the south wall. Light from that long room, the only single-story extension of the house, splashed across the flagstone terrace. Beyond it, casting its own eerie blue glow, was the swimming pool.

Not the situation of someone anticipating real trouble, McLean thought.

Louis had expected advance warning from the gates or his roving patrol.

"I'm going in first," said McLean.

"No!"

"We don't know who or what we're facing. I'm used to this kind of thing, Angie, you're not. I want you where I know you'll be—where I can bring or send Tony to you. If we're lucky, Louis will have locked him in his room. It's the room in the front corner of the east wing, right?

"Yes, but—"

"Give me five minutes. Then get over near the terrace. Stay in the shadows, where you can see what's happening if I come out the back door. Okay?"

In the end she could not deny that this was more his terrain than hers. He could climb more quickly, break and enter more efficiently, if he did not have to look over his shoulder to see if she was there.

"Five minutes," she said. "Take care . . ."

He kissed her quickly on her cool, damp lips and was gone, disappearing silently into the mist.

Five minutes earlier, McLean thought, when Richie left the house to check out the alarm in the woods, there had been no knowledge of immediate danger in the house. No sign of fear. Louis Marchetti had been sitting there in his playroom, out of the rain, smiling in anticipation, lights blazing, his swimming pool lit up in invitation.

Was he still alive?

19

THE WINDOW OF THE BOY'S ROOM was unlocked and open about six inches at the bottom. Its wood-framed screen was old and rusted. McLean, who had reached the window by means of a shaky, vine-covered trellis, listened until he assured himself that the room was empty. Not even the sound of a child's breathing.

Frowning, he punctured the rusty screen with two fingers and released the catch. Setting the screen aside, he hoisted himself into the dark room.

He glanced toward the ground below the window. Nothing stirred. A gentle gust of wind blew rain in his face through the open window.

McLean waited for his eyes to adjust to the deeper interior darkness. The bedroom door stood open but the hall beyond it was also dark. After a long minute he was able to see that the room had not been slept in this night. A few of Tony's clothes were thrown over the back of a chair or scattered on the floor. The bed was undisturbed.

The house had an unnatural stillness. There was a maid, Angie had said, but if custom prevailed she was off on Sunday. Richie, all-around handyman, had probably done the cooking, cleaning, driving and bartending, besides supplying necessary muscle. Well, nobody was good at everything . . .

Louis had been alone in the house, then, when Richie ran out. Louis and Tony. *Where was the boy?*

The hall carpet was thick. McLean's patient footsteps produced no creak or groan. Down the back stairs to the kitchen? No, the kitchen was one of the few lighted rooms.

The main stairway. A carpet runner to muffle his steps. A chandelier hung on a long brass chain from the high ceiling toward the great hall below. McLean circled it on the staircase, heart thudding. He had begun to have a feeling of dread at the pit of his stomach, the fear that he was too late.

Light from Louis's entertainment room fell across the far end of a wide hallway that led to the back of the house. Kitchen off the hall to the right. Another connecting doorway opened into the living room.

McLean slipped through the dark living room, skirting bulky furniture, curtained windows, the distinctive shape of a tall secretary with its writing top open, a grand piano filling one corner.

French doors at the back of the room, their panels of clear glass. A view of the playroom beyond . . .

Louis had filled his entertainment center with a wall of electronics, a wet bar on one side with white plastic stools, Italian modern furnishings lacquered in black and white, a large circular poker table, leagues of black and white floor tiles, and at the far end of the long room, a vintage pool table.

For Louis Marchetti the fun was over.

He lay sprawled face down over the pool table. Dark stains on the green felt were still moist. Louis had no pulse in his neck, but the skin of the dead man's cheek was still warm.

McLean felt the spine prickle that was as old as the caveman, as old as the first stone ax or wooden club.

He felt naked in the brightness of the room, amidst all those sleek black and white polished surfaces.

Louis Marchetti must have given Clark Coffey a bad time for a while. He was a big man, heavy muscled, handsome in a way that had gradually been losing out to the puffiness of self-indulgence. McLean could not see his wounds. There had been no gunshot—he had been killed after Richie left the house, within the last few minutes, and McLean would have heard a shot—so it was a good guess that Coffey had used a knife. A garotte would have been cleaner, but maybe Marchetti surprised Coffey with his resistance. Deflated now in death, he still gave an impression of physical strength.

In the fight he must have angered Coffey. What had been done to him from behind with a pool cue was an act of rage.

Out of control, McLean thought.

He stepped through the sliding glass doors onto the terrace. He didn't have to search for Angie. She stood to the left of the pool, near the top of some flagstone steps that led to the terrace from the garden below. McLean started to say, "Don't go in there. You don't want to . . ."

Angie wasn't listening.

She stared off beyond the pool where—McLean recalled from Angie's sketch—the lawn dropped away in a broad sweep until it came to the stream and the willows drooping over its banks.

And the old mill.

None of this was clearly visible in the rainy darkness. What was visible, drawing the eye like a single illuminated painting in a dark room, was a large panel of light, perhaps ten feet across and six feet high, that seemed to float in mid-air high above the ground.

Centered in that frame of light, teetering at its front edge, was a small boy tied to a straight-backed wooden chair.

"Oh, Louis! My God, how could you—!"

"Not Louis," McLean said quietly behind her.

Her head snapped around. "What do you mean?" The question came out hostile, angry. "How can you know that?"

"Louis is dead."

McLean led Angie from the terrace but not before she had turned toward the house and seen the stomach-lurching image of Louis Marchetti splayed out across the green felt of his pool table. McLean blocked her view and held her, steering her away. She stumbled once going down the steps and onto the path that carried them into protective darkness.

It was a world suddenly turned upside down, where dark was snug and safe, where light was cold and dangerous.

The rain had thinned out until it was little more than a fine mist, cool against the face. It softened and fuzzed images like the filter used on a camera lens to throw a veil over the honest truths of age and wear. Feeling Angie buckle as her stomach heaved, McLean swore softly to himself.

They walked through the mist, invisible themselves now in the deep well of the night, toward the unreal window of light suspended high above the ground. The old stone mill had four or five levels, McLean remembered. The lighted opening was probably at the third or fourth of those levels.

They stopped where a low stone wall defined a path leading

to a plank door set into the front wall of the mill. Angie lifted wet eyes toward the bright rectangle above them and choked back a cry of anger. "Damn Louis! Damn him!"

"Forget Louis," McLean said. "Remember what you felt once, but not what changed it. Tony's the only one who matters now."

"I know but . . . look at him!"

Clark Coffey had rigged a spotlight as if for a photo session. Young Tony sat transfixed on a wooden chair in the center of that harsh beam of light. His head sank forward in an attitude of despair.

"Tony! Oh Tony, baby . . ."

"Mom!" The boy gave a cry of joy. "Mom, where are you?"

As he struggled, unable to break free, the chair rocked at the edge of the opening before him, more than twenty feet above the ground.

"Don't move, honey! Don't move . . ."

"That's right, Tony, don't fight it. We're coming to get you."

"Daddy! I knew you'd come, I just knew it!"

McLean swallowed a lump in his throat. Only in the last few months had Tony begun calling him Daddy. What kind of confusion must now be churning in his brain? How many Daddys could a three-year-old boy have?

McLean saw a shadow cross the frame of light above them and he drew Angie toward the cover of one of the trees near the edge of the stream. Taking a step away from her, he called out, "Coffey? It's me, McLean."

"Yeah, I know. You kinda lucked out there in the woods. That could've been you."

"Or Angie," said McLean. "Is that what you wanted, Coffey? To kill a woman who has nothing to do with you? The boy's mother?"

The taunt brought a brief silence. Then Coffey said—he had

changed position already but was still on one of the upper levels of the mill, his voice floating down through the darkness—"You know fucking well that's not what I get it up for. You're the one brought the woman here. Anything happened to her, it would've been on your head."

"Always blame the other guy," McLean said. "Just like Carl Warner."

"You son of a bitch! You couldn't carry his fucking socks!"

"What are you trying to *do?*" Angie said.

"Give him what he wants. High Noon at midnight. He wants a confrontation. That's what I want him to want."

"You're making him angrier."

"I hope so," said McLean. "Listen to me, Angie. I want you to walk in there now, go up the stairs to where Tony is, and cut him loose."

"I . . . I don't understand. How can I?"

"Coffey won't stop you. Trust me, honey." *Never trust anyone who has to say, "Trust me."*

"It's the one who was at Wanamaker's, isn't it? The one who tried to kill you."

"Yes."

"You knew he'd be here. How could you be sure?"

"I invited him, sort of. I decided to let him know where I'd be tonight. I made a phone call where I was sure he'd get the information. Since he couldn't know what I was planning, his best bet was to get here ahead of me. He did, but not by much."

Her gaze jerked back toward the house at the top of the knoll, the obscene image of Louis Marchetti sprawled across his pool table a vivid memory. "My God!" she murmured. "You *used* him. You used both of them."

"We had two problems. I figured I'd try to cut it down to one. Just get them together and see what happened."

"What if Louis had killed *him*?"

"I didn't think that would happen, but if it had . . . then one of our problems would still have been eliminated. The more dangerous one," he added with a glance upward at the face of the old mill, the fitted stones dark from the rain. "I knew he wouldn't hurt Tony. But I didn't count on him using Tony against me."

"You're a ruthless bastard, aren't you?"

"Where you and Tony are threatened . . . whatever it takes."

She shivered. "I don't understand that man up there. I thought I understood Louis, if recognizing slime means you understand it. But this man . . . Louis never had a chance, did he? Any more than that Richie did."

"Not much chance."

After a brief hard stare her eyes faltered. Her gaze went to the lighted box where Tony was tied to the chair, teetering on the edge of night. Looking away, she had tried to keep McLean from seeing the fear that sprang into her eyes. "Do *you* have a chance?" she whispered.

"I know who and what he is. Louis didn't. Richie didn't. That gives me . . . some kind of chance."

For a time she was silent, trying to come to grips with what seemed an alien world into which she had accidentally strayed. Finally she asked, "How could you be sure he wouldn't harm Tony?"

"Coffey sees himself as a hero," McLean said without hesitation. "He has to justify himself in his own eyes. Heroes kill enemies but they don't harm innocent children. For him Tony is just a . . . a bargaining chip."

"He thinks you're a traitor."

"Yes, I suppose he does."

She was sorting it out, arranging it in her head so it made sense. So it would quiet the racing of her heart, warm the cold trickle along the spine, stop the shivering inside. "Heroes don't harm women either, do they?"

"He's a cowboy. He wears a white hat. Women and children are off limits. I don't think any of that has changed. I think he'll let you go. You and Tony. All he wants is me."

"How do we know that's all he wants?"

"I'll ask him," said McLean.

A row of large willow trees hung over the stream bed. The bank was broken, uneven, exposing big roots. Under the trees the shadows were deeper. Water sifted over them from the drooping foliage.

"When I start talking to him," McLean said, "go back out there in the open, right in front of the door where Coffey can see you. Don't make any sudden moves or do anything else, okay?"

"Okay."

"Can you get up to that third level or whatever it is in the dark?"

"It's the fourth level, counting the bottom where the big water wheel is. And yes, the stairs are right in the middle of the building. I've climbed them a hundred times. Little short flights, open steps with no railing or anything, but I won't have any problem. Besides, once I start climbing there'll be enough light from above so I can see where I am."

"All right, I'm going over there to the other bank. He'll know where I am from my voice. Don't go out where he can see you until you hear me say so."

He touched her wet cheek with one hand, gently, the lightest of caresses while feeling a strange heaviness in his chest. "I love you," he said. "Tell Tony I love him too."

"Oh my God, you think—"

"No, no. Just wanted it on record."

"I love you," she whispered.

"Wouldn't have it any other way."

He left quickly. Taking off his shoes and socks, he left them on the near bank. Barefoot, he crossed the stream and crept through the trees until he came to the edge of a clearing between the trees and the back wall of the old mill.

The huge water wheel was in the corner of the building nearest him, one level down from the entrance on the far side. Glancing upward, McLean was able to see a line of light where a large sliding door was open about an inch.

"Coffey! I'm over here."

His voice didn't sound very loud in the heavy air, but within seconds the sliding door high above him on the back wall of the mill slid open about a foot, letting a bar of light spill out.

"I want to make a deal, Coffey."

"No deals, McLean."

"It's the one you want. Let the boy go, and the woman. They don't mean anything to you. I'm the one you want. Let them go and I'll come to you." He didn't give Coffey time to think over his proposition. It had to be now. "Angie! You can go up now. Take Tony and leave!"

The wait seemed interminable, though it could not have been more than a minute. He couldn't see what was happening on the other side of the mill, or be certain when Angie reached the upper level where Tony was tied to the chair, a small, frightened and bewildered hostage to one man's warped desire for vengeance. He could only listen to the pounding of his heart, and wait . . .

He thought he heard a scuffling of footsteps but could not be certain.

Then silence.

The seconds ticked by, each one a hammer blow in his chest.

"They're gone, McLean. I'm waiting for you."

Relief was physical, driving him to his knees. It was a moment before he stumbled to his feet.

"Don't worry, Coffey . . . I'm coming."

20

THERE WERE SOME THINGS you didn't walk away from. It wasn't just that Clark Coffey had thrown down the gauntlet. It wasn't only the knowledge that, if he turned around and left Coffey to fume impotently in the mill, Coffey might go after Angie and Tony in pure rage.

A deal was a deal.

Besides, McLean wanted the confrontation as badly as Coffey did.

For the last minute, waiting, he had avoided looking up at the light that spilled from the upper level, wanting his eyes to know only the darkness.

At the edge of his vision he was aware of the light suddenly winking out, as if blotted up by the dark.

He ran toward the southwest corner of the mill and ducked through the large opening above the stream.

There was just enough light from outside to make the massive wheel's outlines detectable. Even motionless it conveyed a sense of power banked and waiting. From it a system of meshing gears with giant wooden teeth pushed rods and pulleys, belts and ropes and chains upward through a hole in the ceiling and on through the different levels of the mill, changing directions and point of application of the pushing or pulling force as needed. The whole awakened admiration for those who had created it a hundred and fifty years ago without the aid of a single computer graphic.

McLean crept up a wide ramp past the wheel to his left and, to his right, a small adjoining room that contained an electric generator. It was an auxiliary power source, Angie had explained, to call on when there was a drought and water power by itself was inadequate. Not like the good old days, McLean had thought, when a dried-up stream meant that your grain was simply not ground.

McLean reached the second level. A shaft beside him rose into a dark hole above. McLean ducked away. The hole was like an eye staring down. Or the muzzle of a gun.

He crouched next to a scarred wooden counter. The wood had a smell shared by the mill—an old, familiar, musty smell seasoned by the dust of flour ground long ago that coated floors and surfaces. The rain dripped outside and the chill seeped through the walls.

McLean made out the first flight of narrow steps. Could he chance them? His senses, reaching out like antennae along the dark aisles and into the bins and storage places, told him that Coffey was not here, not on this level.

He went up the steps, barefoot, silent as dust.

At the next level he waited again, listening. He was beginning to see better in the pitch blackness inside the mill. But there

was plenty of cover here. Partitions, shafts and chutes and
elevators, tables and bins, posts and beams all created their own
pools of darkness.

His nostrils twitched. Dust drifted in the still air.

Dust filtered down when it settled. Coffey was still above him.

McLean was now at the third level. Another short flight of
steps climbed to the fourth level, where Tony had been staked
out as bait.

Coffey was waiting.

McLean retreated from the stairway down a narrow aisle. More
by touch than sight he found one of the open chutes that extended
up through the ceiling. Silently, every nerve screaming, he
began to climb. The opening at the top was just large enough to
scrape through.

He poked head and shoulders through, like a gopher peering
out of his hole. He waited, listening, sniffing the air for any
disturbance.

He felt movement even before he heard it. Pulled head and
shoulders down like a turtle withdrawing into its shell. Let
himself drop in a free fall, sliding down the chute.

A glancing blow caught one arm before it cleared the opening
in the ceiling. Something thudded against the plank floor above
him as he dropped clear, the blow so solid and heavy the floor
shook and the whole building picked up the vibration and shuddered.

McLean tumbled to the lower level. As he hit the floor he
rolled away from the chute. A whine close to his ear was like a
gnat or mosquito. He hadn't heard the shot.

He scuttled like an animal through the darkness. His own
gun was in his hand without his knowing how it had gotten there.
The body and brain worked out their own signals in a crisis,
leaving the *me* out of it, like a running back seeing the seam,
turning and slashing through the opening without conscious

decision. *Something that can't be taught*, the coaches always said. *Either you have it or you don't*.

The killing instinct, too.

Resting in a corner, McLean considered the tactical situation. Coffey had had time to scout the mill. There had been no time to do so *after* he had killed Louis Marchetti, just minutes before McLean found him. But he must have been here earlier. How else explain the dramatic lighting setup with Tony at center stage?

Coffey had *chosen* the mill for their meeting, McLean thought with a chill. He had explored it, memorized its ways. He had had time to create other booby traps.

He heard a small scurrying sound, like a rat scuttling among the rafters. Turning his head toward the sound, he saw a red muzzle flash.

Too late, McLean ducked instinctively. But the blind shot thunked into wood two feet from his head.

The shot had come from another of the myriad openings in the floors of the building that accommodated shafts and chutes and elevators.

Coffey's terrain, McLean acknowledged.

He had to change it.

How to do so without drawing more fire? Coffey had heard and reacted to the slightest movement, whether a stirring of dust or the scrape of cloth against rough wood.

Create more sound, McLean thought. How do you make one sound unheard? Create chaos . . .

He remembered the electric generator.

Describing the old mill with enthusiasm, Angie had gone into more detail than had seemed necessary at the time. McLean thought of the elaborate system of gears and drives and pulleys, the meshing of giant teeth, the slap and grate and rub of leather belts, of straps and ropes, the grinding of wheels and rollers . . .

The mill was still a functioning mill, Angie had said, when Marchetti bought the place just a few years ago. The sellers had turned the noisy system on for them. "It really puts on a show!" she had said.

Marchetti must have turned it on for others, McLean thought. To show it off.

All McLean had to do was find his way back to the generator. Find the switch. Get to it without being killed along the way.

Angie and Tony were safe by now. He felt an odd kind of serenity, his earlier fears having ebbed away. Serenity while trapped in a dark building with a trained killer who was out of control. He thought about Gary Cooper as the sheriff in *High Noon*, going out into the street with his gun, alone. McLean had Angie and Tony with him all the way. The sheriff's bride, Grace Kelly, hadn't really bailed out on him; she was there for him at the end. But the beleaguered sheriff didn't know that. He thought she had let him down, that he was facing his High Noon alone.

Whatever happened, for the first time in his life McLean knew that he was not alone.

He decided he would never make it back down the steps in the center of the building. And he would not go undetected for long if he tried to crawl along the floor among the warren of bins and tables and chutes.

Elevators, he thought.

An elevator meant a shaft. But would there be a shaft large enough to accommodate a human body? Would the shaft be clear, or did that depend on where the cages were?

Cautiously he lifted his head and peered around.

He was crouching only an arm's length from an open elevator shaft.

The cage was above him, perhaps at eye level if he stood.

The shaft itself was only a black hole in blackness. Tracing its outline with the tips of his fingers—no scratching fingernails to set the teeth on edge—he found that it was more or less square. And barely big enough.

Coffey would know the moment he dropped into the shaft. It had to be quick, hold your breath and dive in.

Groping blindly, he found a pair of ropes at the back of the shaft. He eased out of his crouch and slipped his legs into the opening. He could feel cooler air from the shaft below. He let his weight transfer to the ropes and felt one of them give way completely. The cage above him suddenly tipped over and McLean was drowning in flour.

Coffey's shout of triumph echoed in his ears as he plummeted down the shaft, coughing and choking, blind with the flour in his eyes. His head bumped hard. His back scraped the narrow shaft and a sharp pain struck his left shoulder.

Tumbling out of the shaft onto the lower level, McLean knew that he had only moments to live. Coffey's booby trap had not only left him blind and demoralized, but he had also lost his gun during his ride down the shaft. He could hear Coffey's footsteps pounding down the steps after him. Another gleeful shout——"McLean? How do you like it, McLean?"

He brushed flour from his eyelashes and his eyes and cheeks. A wash of paler air appeared. The open wall behind the water wheel! He stumbled to his feet. Pawed at the flour half-blinding him. Heard Coffey's steps hit the top of the steps at the level just above him.

He ran blindly and heard Coffey shout as he missed a step in the darkness and tumbled down the steps.

The fall gave McLean the time he needed. The generator room was little more than a closet off a ramp near the big water wheel. The door resisted his tug. He jerked it open with a screech of wood splintering.

In the small dark room he slapped the walls, searching frantically for a switch panel. He could feel the pressure of Coffey's reckless pursuit like a crushing weight. No switch, no panel, nothing! The walls were blank on both sides and behind the generator. Where was the goddamn switch?

His fingers brushed across it. It was mounted on the generator itself.

McLean heard Coffey jump from the steps. The floor shuddered as steps pounded toward him. Almost on top of him.

McLean sucked in a breath and hit the switch.

He got what he wanted.

He awakened chaos.

It really puts on a show! Angie had said. In broad daylight the hubbub might have seemed normal. In the darkness of this rainy, overcast night it was magnified a hundredfold, a stupendous roaring and grinding and pounding turmoil contained and magnified within the foreshortened levels and crowded aisles of the old mill.

McLean—even though he had been prepared for the uproar— felt like a pedestrian trapped in the middle of the freeway in the dark.

He tried to blank out the furor. Though he had known what was coming, he couldn't shut it out. The roar took over his brain, making it almost impossible to think.

Where had Coffey gone? The noise, so unexpected and terrifying, had panicked him, driven him back. He had retreated back up the steps.

Everything seemed out of control—like Clark Coffey.

How would this affect him? How would a mind threatened by its own chaos respond to Chaos itself?

McLean moved through it with an effort of will, jumping and flinching as unseen forces chugged past him in the blackness or seemed to hurtle toward him. He had reached the second level before he heard, above the building's uproar, Clark Coffey's endless scream.

It came from almost directly overhead. McLean found the steps at the center of the building. He went up them bent over and feeling for each step with one hand. A leather belt, frayed at its edges, slapped at him in passing.

At the third level Coffey emptied his gun—firing shots not at McLean but at an elevator cage that trundled from a shaft and spilled a load of air into an empty chute.

"Coffey!" McLean shouted. "I'm here!"

He saw the pale round moon of Coffey's face turn toward him, the open mouth a dark circle within a circle.

Coffey pulled the trigger of his empty gun. In a pantomime of rage he hurled the gun at the sound of McLean's voice. It clattered down the steps.

Coffey broke.

He ran toward the side of the mill. Blundering into a counter, he bounced off it and kept going. As McLean started after the fleeing shadow, Coffey slid a big door open, its wheels rumbling on an overhead track. A pale ghost of rain-washed air blew in. And in that instant, McLean saw Coffey clearly, saw Coffey swing to face him, saw him shouting against the ongoing clamor of the mill's antique machinery—a clamor that diminished perceptibly with the door open wide to let in some light and air while the imprisoned sound spilled out.

For an instant Coffey disappeared from the opening. When McLean saw him again he was brought up short.

Coffey had planned this confrontation carefully. His empty pistol had bounced down the steps, but he had been prepared for such an emergency and even in his panicked state his training surfaced. The weapon that now appeared in his hands was compact and ugly and worked with a legendary efficiency: an Uzi submachine gun.

The chatter of the Uzi was barely audible in the surrounding turmoil. It was the muzzle flashes that made McLean hit the floor. The shots went high and wild.

A second burst came closer.

McLean's hand closed around a length of wood, smooth and round like a handle of some kind. As another tracery of bullets from the Uzi slapped a partition above his head, McLean hurled the wooden club.

It struck Coffey in the shoulder, staggering him. He wobbled at the edge of the opening, as Tony had earlier teetered in his chair. And a spotlight from ground level stabbed upward, silhouetting Coffey starkly against the light much as Tony had been caught.

Coffey spun around. He fired at the light. Something plucked at him, jerking him this way and that, so that he seemed to be dancing at the apron of a stage.

Just before another burst from the Uzi put out the spotlight, Coffey's dancing steps missed a beat.

Then chaos shut down as suddenly as it had started.

The silence screamed.

Clark Coffey didn't fall or jump. He simply rushed out into the night, the Uzi on full automatic spraying random violence into the darkness, Coffey charging into the face of the enemy, in his own mind a hero to the last.

He dropped from sight.

From below came a single, meaningless shot.

Then a deeper silence.

All McLean could think of, reliving in that frozen moment of time the memory of Carl Warner's death long ago in a stifling hotel room in South Africa, all McLean thought was, *I didn't kill him, after all.*

* * *

Figures moved in the darkness as McLean emerged from the mill. Some lights came on behind him and a flashlight wavered near a group standing motionless beside a crumpled figure on the ground.

Eric Zeller detached himself from the group and approached McLean without haste. He was hatless in the rain, the collar of his coat turned up.

The two men regarded each other in silence, without surprise. McLean nodded toward Coffey. "He forgot about the cavalry."

"What's that?"

"Coffey. He liked playing Cowboys and Indians. I guess he forgot about the cavalry showing up at the end."

"I suppose that means something cryptic," said Zeller. "I'm surprised you haven't asked what kept me."

"What kept you?"

"Some idiot in a red pickup with a battering ram on the front end skidded around a corner and slammed into us. If I ever catch the son of a bitch . . ." He broke off when McLean started laughing. "What's so funny?"

"You . . . in a ditch . . . in the rain . . ."

Zeller waited until McLean had sobered before he said, "You could have waited for us."

"Played it safe . . . yes, I know. But that's what I've been doing the past three years. I found out that playing it safe doesn't make it safe." McLean paused. "By the way, how did you find out about tonight?" When Zeller appeared reluctant to answer, he added, "I know about Paul Thornton tipping Coffey off."

Zeller nodded. "So that's why you made a point of spelling out where you were going to be tonight when you talked to Paul."

"Yes."

"You knew we had his phone tapped?"

"It seemed probable."

"Mmm. I've suspected for some time that Thornton was involved. Misplaced loyalty," Zeller added with distaste. He was not angry. His reaction was that of a pastry chef discovering that someone has used a prepared cake mix.

"What will happen with him?"

"You mean, will he be cashiered in disgrace? Hardly." Zeller did not need to point out that a large percentage of those in the Agency would be sympathetic to both Coffey and Thornton. "He will be allowed to choose his own course."

McLean understood. Thornton would not be publicly disciplined or fired; he would simply become irrelevant, his career put on permanent hold. When the truth became clear enough, his position uncomfortable enough, he would voluntarily retire. In this respect the Agency functioned much like any large corporation.

McLean peered past Zeller. The rain had almost stopped and he could see the dark ribbon of the service road at the bottom of the broad sweep of lawn. Zeller said, "Those London publishers of yours . . . they had a burglary the other day, did you hear?"

"No."

"The thieves didn't get much. They did, however, steal one manuscript."

The words caught McLean's attention. He remained silent, too drained for anger.

"You misled me, Barney, about that book of yours."

"Did I?"

"You know damned well you did. You led me to understand that you'd written a muckraking, whistle-blowing epic. But it isn't that at all, is it?"

"I tried to write an honest account of a dishonest profession."

"Mmm. The thieves didn't think much of it, apparently. The manuscript was read and discarded. Your publishers found it in their trash a couple of days later. Not very exciting stuff, honesty.

You did have a few criticisms of the Agency in there. But some important incidents were not even mentioned . . ."

"Only individual aberrations that would have distorted the picture," McLean said impatiently. Still no activity on the service road. "And done more harm than good."

Zeller nodded. "Yes, of course. If your publishers . . . that is, if the book should be submitted to an American publisher . . ."

"Yes?"

"We would not object."

Staring past him down the slope, McLean saw the red Datsun pickup. It skidded to a stop below the stables, its rear end fishtailing as the small truck spun on the rain-slick road. The side door opened and Angie jumped out of the cab. Tony tumbled from the seat after her.

Zeller followed his gaze. If he recognized the Datsun with the battering ram mounted on the front bumper, he gave no indication. He said, "You'll be going back to Fortune, Barney? I don't think you need fear any more reprisals . . . anything from the past."

"That's something we'll decide together," said McLean. "We're a family now."

He went past Eric Zeller and started down the hill without a backward glance.